URBAN SHOTS
FIRST COLLECTION

Paritosh Uttam is a software professional and a writer by passion. He is an engineering graduate from IIT Madras and IISc Bangalore. His first novel *Dreams in Prussian Blue* was published in 2010. He lives in Pune with his wife, Smita, and son, Palash. More at www.paritoshuttam.com

URBAN SHOTS
FIRST COLLECTION

Edited by
Paritosh Uttam

RUPA

To all the young writers out there
who aspire to tell beautiful stories.

Published by
Rupa Publications India Pvt. Ltd 2014
7/16, Ansari Road, Daryaganj
New Delhi 110002

Sales centres:
Allahabad Bengaluru Chennai
Hyderabad Jaipur Kathmandu
Kolkata Mumbai

ISBN: 978-81-291-2987-1

First impression 2014

10 9 8 7 6 5 4 3 2 1

The moral right of the author has been asserted.

Contents

Foreword

When well-known author, Ahmed Faiyaz called, asking if I could write the foreword for this book, I was delighted at the idea of introducing urban tales of love, regret, acceptance, and every other supposedly 'urban' feeling that one could write about. You might ask what makes such a theme relevant for an entire anthology to be based on. Go read it for yourself and you will understand the relevance and need for a book with such an honest portrayal of the world around us. An unskewed reality.

This volume offers its readers a collection of wonderful, carefully picked stories that talk about different aspects of urban life varying from relationships, lifestyles, love, depression, domestic violence, longing and friendship. From the sweetness of 'Apple Pies and a Grey Sweater' shared with a lover, to the 'Liberation' felt by a woman torn by the rural-urban conflict, from coming to grip a sense of loss in 'Effacing Memories' to dealing with loss and moving on in 'Hope Comes in Small Packages', stories in this collection explore life from every possible perspective. You will see society from the eyes of a child, a lover, a wife, a mother, a friend. The emotions expressed envelop you as you read each word, leaving you in awe of the unknown, or fascinated with the familiar. The familiar 'Cup of Tea' that you come home to will bring about a feeling varying greatly from the sense of infidelity that 'Morning Showers' would bring. What truly makes it great is the universal theme of urban life, which is easy to relate to and thereby, draws the reader into these short stories by Indian writers like Paritosh Uttam, Bishwanath Ghosh, Prateek Gupta, Sahil Khan, Kainaz Motivala, Malathi Jaikumar, Ahmed Faiyaz, Abha Iyengar, Vrinda Baliga, and many others.

Imagine yourself standing in a crowded bus, trying hard to look out of the window to catch ephemeral glimpses of the street lights, of busy roads, of traffic jams. You are in the midst of it all, brushing shoulders with strangers who have their own stories to tell. This book is that window in the bus, giving you an insight into the fictional or non-fictional lives of others. The Editorial Team at Grey Oak has done an excellent job in choosing these specific stories. Though the stories are starkly different from each other, there is a certain flow that makes for an easy read. You would not want to put down the book and say that you have had enough for the day even if you're half way through it. The stories vary in the time they are set in, the age group of the characters, their pace, in the different voices that narrate the stories, and in the number of words used to convey the struggles and ways to deal with loss, unrequited love, friendship, longing, monotony of urban life, and even the vicious cycle of marriage. Turn the pages and enter the weird and wonderful urban world the way these writers see it, keeping aside all preconceived notions, clichés, and any emotional baggage you may have, since you'll be having enough of theirs to carry on your shoulders.

Rohini Kejriwal is a nineteen-year-old wanderer exploring life as she knows it. She is an aspiring writer, and loves photography

and listening to music. Her writing can be found on http://
revelationswithin. blogspot.com

Relationships

Hope Comes in Small Packages

KAINAZ MOTIVALA

It's my first show as a designer. I have Bollywood actors Seema Singh and Sanjay Rampal walking the ramp to showcase my new collection. Life couldn't be better—a bright, promising start as an independent designer, Sumit's love, and our baby on the way. I collapse five minutes before I am to go and take a bow on the ramp. All I feel is excruciating pain. I wake up in an ambulance.

It's a dark and stormy September night, Sumit is holding my hand, telling me that everything will be alright. 'Be brave, I promise you we'll be there soon.'

He looks nervous and types furiously on his mobile. I can hear the blaring of horns and the sound of the pouring rain on the roof of the ambulance; we are stuck in the crazy Mumbai traffic. I'm writhing in pain but my screams are drowned by the blaring loudspeakers playing Hindi film songs; the roads are blocked by people heading towards the sea to immerse their Ganesh idols. My condition gets worse with every agonizing moment. My water bag burst an hour ago and we were rushed from the Marriot towards Lilavati Hospital, trying desperately to get to the emergency room as fast as possible. I scream, grab Sumit's hand and ask him to save me and our baby. The blinding pain is too much for me to bear; I close my eyes and drift into the darkness.

When I open my eyes next, the music's gone, the car horns have stopped blaring and I am in what looks like a hospital room; plain white walls and the sickening, unmistakable smell of a hospital. Sumit is by my side, rubbing my hand, before taking it to his lips and kissing it. He appears tense. A wave of panic suddenly overcomes me, I realize that the pain is now gone. I look at him with searching eyes, he looks away. 'What happened Sumit?'

He seems hesitant, there's an aggrieved expression on his face. 'I'm glad that you've regained consciousness. We got you to the hospital and the doctors had to perform an emergency C-section. The baby was in distress. The umbilical cord was wrapped around his neck....' he trails off.

'I don't understand, I had two more months. Is he alright? Where is he? I need to see him.' I leaned forward and tugged at his collar, imploring for an answer.

A tear rolls down Sumit's cheek, 'He didn't make it love, we didn't make it in time...I'm sorry.' He gets into bed next to me and hugs me.

I can't make sense of his words, I must have heard wrong. This can't be happening to me. I get out of bed and rush towards the nurse standing at a distance, with a small white bundle. He's in her arms, sleeping silently, never to stir again, wrapped in a white cloth. I snatch the bundle from her and look at his tiny face. He looks so peaceful, my little angel. The nurse tries to take him back, I touch his little fingers and they're as cold as ice. I shake him, I wail, but he doesn't open his eyes or cry.

'Priya! Priya, wake up!' I opened my eyes with a start. I was covered in sweat, screaming, and trembling violently.

Sumit held me down, 'Did you dream about it again?' It all slowly sinks in, I'm in my bedroom at home and this happened a year ago. It's the same nightmare, playing all over again. It started and ended in the same way. I lost my baby. I looked at Sumit's troubled face. 'Priya, it's been a year now. Listen to me, you've got to get over it honey. This isn't good for us; it doesn't work for you or me. It doesn't change what happened. We cannot undo destiny.'

How can he be saying such things, how can he not understand what I'm going through? I lost my child, it was his child too. What does he mean by it doesn't work for us? How do you ever get over holding your baby's limp body in your arms?

'Talk to me Priya. It's going to help if we can talk about this. Remember what the doctor sa....'

'There's nothing you can do to help. You must be tired, go to sleep. Sorry you had to wake up.'

I switched off the light and turned away from him. He can't understand my pain, there's no point talking to him. This is my loss and my problem. The pain I feel is mine alone.

Not much had changed since that fateful night. It was still raining outside and I can hear the loud Ganpati music playing in the distance. There was just one painful, terrible difference: Last year I had been waiting eagerly for this day to come and this year I was dreading it more than I had ever dreaded anything in my life. It would have been my son's first birthday. My little boy, with his small nose, tiny fingers and tiny toes. My own little Sameer!

I lay back in bed and fantasized about holding my angel in my arms, smelling his sweet baby scent, watching him take his first steps, listen to him babble. These magical moments are the only thing I lived for but then reality always came back to haunt me. I could feel the tears pricking at the back of my eyes, threatening to flow again. I will never hear him gurgle and call my name. I will never see him crawl or see him stand. I won't see him riding a cycle around the building like other kids. There won't be a first day at school or a graduation day. I won't see him write and I won't see him talk. I won't hear the words 'Momma I won!' I won't see the pride in Sumit's eyes when my boy conquers the world. I shut my eyes tightly, trying hard to fight the tears but then the agony takes over and I let them spill. I didn't know if I believed in his existence anymore, but I prayed to God to make this go away, to let me feel something other than pain, to bring some miracle into my life.

I heard Sumit stir in his sleep, I got up from the bed and walked towards the window, I didn't want my sobs to wake him up again. The pitiful expression he had on his face when he looked at me, bothered me. I don't need pity, I needed understanding. How do I get over this overwhelming sense of grief? I walked out to the balcony and put my head out, letting the raindrops touch my face. I liked it when it poured incessantly, when the rain Gods lashed down on our chaotic planet, it made me feel like the skies were crying with me and that thought was oddly comforting.

A shrill cry shook me out of my petulant stupor; I couldn't tell where or from whom it was coming. I listened carefully, and soon I heard it again, this time I realized it was a little pup yelping, but I still couldn't see him. I craned my head out of the balcony even further, and then saw the most painful thing ever—a little newborn puppy was lying next to his mother who lay there, dead to the world, as still as a rock. It was shivering, and whining at the touch of the icy raindrops and thundering skies. On a dark, stormy night, it was helpless and alone.

Watching him lie there, and wail helplessly made me feel terrible about his plight. Something stirred inside me and I ran to get a blanket. I switched on the light in the room and this woke Sumit, but I wasn't concerned about it this time. Taking an old blanket and my umbrella, I rushed out of the room.

'What is it now Priya? What are you doing?'

'Nothing Sumit, just go back to sleep.' I slipped on a robe and ran out of the door. I could hear Sumit's footsteps behind me. He got out of bed and followed me downstairs. 'Priya, what's gotten into you? Where are you going at this time? It's raining outside!'

'Rain', 'Puppy' is all I managed as I ran down the stairs all the way from the third floor. I reached the ground floor and ran towards the old garage of the building that I could see from my bedroom balcony. There he was, a little ball of brown fur, whimpering and trembling in the darkness of an unforgiving stormy night. I walked up to him, and after looking up at me with his sad eyes, imploring to do something about his mother, he instinctively pushed himself closer to her. His fear was palpable. I bent down next to him and touched him lightly on his head to comfort him. Instead he recoiled and let out a shrill mourn. I took a step back but remained close enough.

'Come on honey, we can leave him in the watchman's room. Let's go up and get some sleep,' said Sumit who had followed me down. I ignored him.

I moved closer to the pup and held the umbrella over him and his mother's limp body. Minutes passed by and he seemed to realize that I meant no harm. I reached out and picked him up. This time he didn't struggle. I realized how small he was—no bigger than the palm of my hand. I could hear his quiet protests in his silence as I tucked him in the blanket and took him home. Sumit just stood beside me through this, looking dumfounded. He followed me up the stairs without saying a word.

After bringing him home, I wiped the puppy dry before putting him on the rug next to my bed. I assumed he might be hungry so I brought him some milk in a bowl, which he quickly lapped up, licking the bowl dry and then over turning it with his paws. He looked up to me for approval, which brought a faint smile to my face. He wobbled around his new surroundings like a dazed boxer, and then settled down on the rug, the warmth of which he seemed to like. An hour turned into two as I sat watching him twist and turn, and yelp with delight. I turned around to look at the wall clock, it was past two, and I noticed that Sumit was still sitting beside me, watching the puppy too. 'You're not sleeping? You have to go to office tomorrow, right?'

'No, tomorrow's Saturday and besides, it is nice to sit and see the Priya I once knew.'

He smiled gently, the smile he'd flashed me the first time we sat together in literature class, the smile I'd fallen in love with, the smile I had forgotten for a long time! Just as I began drifting away into my memories of a distant past, Sumit jumped up from where he was sitting, a couple of feet away from the puppy, 'Oh God, he just peed on the rug, what a mess!' Looking at his comical expression made me laugh, which seemed to surprise Sumit but then he broke into a laugh too, while the little culprit looked at us innocently sticking his tongue out.

After rinsing the rug, I came back to see that Sumit had gone to bed, and the puppy was rolling around on the floor in the living room. He'll grow tired and fall asleep, I thought. I crept in next to Sumit, who was snoring loudly, and snuggled closer to him, realizing how tired I felt. Moments later, while I tried to fall asleep, I heard a panting sound and a slight whimper. I sat up to see the puppy sitting next to my bed, on the floor, looking at me with his doe eyes, please take me in your arms, they said.

I removed my sheet and got out of bed to pick him up. He whimpered with delight and nuzzled closer to me, 'come here sweetheart,' I said, before kissing his soft head. 'It's late, you should try to sleep.' I set him down on a cushion next to me and lay down watching him; an unspoken bond had formed between us, we kept watching each other for a long time, till he fell asleep.

The next morning I woke up to find Sumit holding the little puppy and whispering something in his ear. 'What are you doing Sumit?' I asked, looking puzzled.

'Guy talk,' he said with a grin. 'Shut up! Tell me ...'

'Just thanking him for making you smile,' he said as he came up to me, and kissed me on my cheek. We put our arms around each other and embraced. I couldn't remember the last time we had hugged, but all I could think about is how warm and safe I felt in his strong arms, and I suddenly realized how much I had missed him. I felt pangs of guilt for ignoring him and keeping him up late.

'It's early, why don't you get some sleep?' he said as he planted another kiss on my forehead.

'That's a good idea,' I said, as I turned my gaze to the little one who lay there looking at me intently. I slept well for the first time in months, only to be woken up by a foul smell. I woke up and saw that the little puppy had made the whole house his toilet!

I got up from the bed and saw Sumit helping the Bai clean up after the puppy. I saw the newspaper lying on the floor, shredded to bits. Sumit was spraying room freshener all over the place trying to get rid of the stench. I couldn't help but smile and thought to myself that he would have made a great father. Just then Sumit noticed me in the hall and smiled, 'Good morning Priya, I'm glad you went back to sleep.'

'Yes I did, it looks like we've been hit by a tornado,' I smiled. I saw the puppy running from one end of the couch to the other, battling with the cushions, biting them, tumbling over them. He saw me and stopped—*I didn't do anything*—his eyes said.

'Yup, he's quite a brat! He was squeaking in the morning, that's how I woke up. He wanted to be fed. Oh and you must know he has rich taste, he doesn't drink water, he only likes milk,' Sumit chuckled.

Just then the puppy came running out of nowhere and started nibbling on my toes. We took him and set him down on the floor next to us, as Shanta bai grumblingly served us breakfast. The pup was set to destroy the squeaky clean order of the house she maintained.

'Shanta bai, please get some milk for him and some bread too,' I said, while Sumit looked at me with a grin.

'I'm keeping him,' I insisted.

'Yes ma'am. So, what do we call him? Lucifer, considering he's a little devil?' Sumit chuckled.

'No he's adorable,' I said looking in his eyes as he looked right back at mine.

'Chestnut?'

'He's not a squirrel.'

'How about Cassidy? It's funny.'

'Ha ha, no thanks Bubba,' I said making a face at him, as the pup gleefully rolled over.

'Custard?'

'Ugh...'

'Shaggy? Snoopy?'

'You've been watching Cartoon Network?'

'Curly? Fudge?'

'Nay.'

'I got it, how about Yoda?'

'Don't go all Star Wars on him, poor baby.' I was thoroughly enjoying our little banter.

'Maybe Chandler from Friends, you like him don't you?'

'He doesn't look like a fast-talking, funny joke-a minute smart ass!'

'I got it. Let's call him Friday?'

'No thanks, Robinson Crusoe. I'm not going to let you take him and disappear on some island,' I chided him mockingly, as I sipped my coffee. Sumit sat back thinking hard, watching our new friend rip apart slices of bread on the floor. Shanta bai stood silently in the background as nobody was listening to her tirade against the pup.

'Maybe Indy? He doesn't seem like he'll listen.' There was an unspoken bond between us, every time I looked at him, every time I said something, I got undivided attention.

'He'll listen to me,' I said saucily, 'won't you my little Hope?'

He sat up and whimpered in delight.

'Hope? It's perfect,' Sumit said excitedly.

'Yes, Hope is perfect,' I smiled and looked down at little Hope, who was happily nibbling away at my toes again.

I normally woke up past eleven, but with Hope around I was up at seven, giving him milk and seeing Sumit off to work, just like the old days. My next few days were spent fussing over Hope, bathing him, feeding him, playing with him and wrestling with him. Yes, wrestling because he was more than willing to chew on absolutely anything in sight. Sumit woke up one Monday morning to see his black Metro shoes with canine bite marks on the soles. He had already mauled two of my shoes while I wasn't looking. We had also found a way to communicate with each other. Every time Hope needed to 'go', he'd look at me with a certain almost apologetic expression, as if to warn me and then he'd circle around a spot before he decided to do his thing. As soon as he gave me 'the look', I would run to get a newspaper and put it under him before he decided to take a dump on the carpet. I quickly learnt that bathing Hope was a huge task. I had heard that dogs don't particularly enjoy baths, but it's different when you really experience it. As I poured water over his tiny body, he scrambled out of the bathroom, leaving small droplets of water all over my bedroom floor. When I finally caught up with him, he looked up at me with a 'you're subjecting me to torture' expression. But by now I'd known Hope long enough to know better than to fall for his cute, innocent expressions. I carried him back into the bathroom, where he struggled hard to free himself from my grip. I quickly soaped him, all the while keeping my feet tightly around him so he couldn't escape again. When we were finally done, he shook himself hard and sprayed me with water. 'Hope! You little brat,' I said in mock anger. How do you like that? he seemed to say yelping with joy. It was his way of getting back at me, I thought. I came and sat down on the bed to catch my breath. Bathing Hope had been more exhausting than I could ever have imagined! The shower seemed to have relaxed my little hyperactive puppy and he decided to settle in for an afternoon siesta. I took this opportunity to take a short nap myself, bathing him had almost been like a little workout for me.

Two hours later, I woke up with a start as I heard a huge crash. I ran into the living room to see what had happened only to realize that little Hope was at it again, with his fun and games, this time he'd managed to topple over a flower vase. 'You're such a naughty little brat! Where do you find the energy to be so destructive?' I asked him as I cleared up the mess. He followed me to the kitchen and looked at me like he had nothing to do with it. As if the wind was responsible for the crash and he actually tried to prevent it. Some try, given that I saw him rip apart the flower petals from the stems with my own eyes.

The next day he was due for his shots so I put him in the car and drove him to the vet. I parked outside the clinic and scooped him up in my arms. As we walked through the clinic, I felt him grow tense and fidgety in my arms; he had never been around so many dogs and was a little intimidated by the bigger ones in the room. It felt nice when he snuggled up to me, and looked at me for protection. When the doctor gave him his shot, he jumped a little in my arms and let out a shrill cry. I hugged him, petted and comforted him. I also gave him some ice-cream for being a good boy and he happily lapped it up and soon forgot about the injection. He sat down and watched me finish mine, looking like he wanted another one for himself.

Now that he was vaccinated, I could take him for a stroll in the park and finally potty train him. My running-with-the-newspaper days were finally over. So every day, we went to the park near my house and played 'fetch' and he absolutely loved it. Every time I threw the ball, he'd run at lightning speed to fetch it and would proudly come back with it and look for my approval. A couple of times he even came back with a tennis ball that belonged to the kids in the park. He tried to play fielder in their game of cricket. He soon had a bunch of ten year olds chasing him around the park, wanting their ball back. He chased squirrels and pigeons, trying to show them that he was the tough guy. It fascinated me how happy something so simple made him, it was pure unadulterated joy. I could just sit for hours and watch him play without getting tired. Just the sight of him, and his pure, fun-loving nature raised my spirits. He had this cuteness about him, in his state of perpetual bliss and mischief.

Sumit came home early one evening and brought me the purple and white orchids that I love and a bottle of my favourite white wine. I tugged at his shirt pulling him closer. I playfully removed his tie and unbuttoned his collar. He kissed me on my nose to which I smiled gleefully. 'It's still my favourite part of you,' he said.

We ordered dinner from an Italian restaurant we used to

frequent when we were dating. While Sumit was freshening up, I set up a candle in the centre of the table with the orchids on either side. When he came out of the shower and saw the impromptu arrangement, he seemed pleased.

'This is perfect Priya, the only thing missing is this...' he said; as he walked up to the music player and played 'Stand by me', our song! He walked up to me, took me in his arms, looked deep into my eyes and said, 'Dance with me.'

I put my head on his shoulder, let the music fill me and let him lead me to the beat of the song. It felt romantic; something I hadn't felt in a while. I was in Sumit's arm, my personal heaven, my perfect place on earth to be. I felt something tugging at my jeans and looked down to find Hope desperately trying to get my attention. Sumit looked at him and laughed. 'Now I know where the term dog in the manger came from.' He scooped him up in his arms, and the three of us swayed to the soft, comforting music.

A week later was Sumit's thirtieth birthday and I decided to throw him a surprise party at home.

'What do you think about a surprise party?'

Hope got up from his lazy slumber and bounced towards me.

'Okay, okay. Let's go and get a nice cake.' He got his paws off my lap and leapt towards the door.

I invited our closest friends, including my best friend, Sudha and her husband, Vikas. Sudha and I had met during our fashion designing course and had hit it off instantly. We had been joined at the hip ever since, but I hadn't seen her for a while.

'Hey Pri. It's been ages,' she said. 'What a pleasant surprise!' I hadn't kept in touch as much and I was bad at returning calls.

'Yes, I know. We need to spend a day together to catch up. Listen I'm at Cakes and More, buying something for Sumit's surprise birthday party. Do you think you can come? And rope in the gang too? I know it's last min…'

'Of course! Don't be silly, wouldn't miss it! What cake are you getting?'

'I thought a nice blueberry cheese cake, just the kind Sumit likes.'

'Nice, I'll see you on Friday then. We'll all be there by six.'

Hope and I also got some snacks and drinks for the party before getting home. Everybody expected me to make my famous mutton biryani so I got all the stuff I needed for it. Hope seemed to be feeling a little left out so I took him to the pet store and suddenly his tail was wagging and he was enthusiastic again, it really didn't take much to make the little one happy. I undid his leash and he leapt towards the little treats shaped like bones. 'You like this?'I asked. He answered with a big swoosh of his tail and I could see the drool dripping from his mouth. He was always hungry, the little devil! He also seemed fascinated by a pink tutu in the store window so I picked that for him. 'You're a cross-dresser, you know that?'

I laughed. He responded by licking my nose.

I called Sumit while he was at the office on Friday. 'Hi honey, so will you come home and pick me up? I'll be ready to leave for dinner,' I said. He had no idea I had planned the party for him and that made it even more exciting. I got busy with the cooking and cleaning and before I knew it, it was already 3.00 p.m. I quickly showered, left Hope in Shanta bai's care and went to the salon to get my hair done. I wanted to look good for Sumit. By the time I got home, it was around five. I changed into the red halter dress I had designed, which Sumit had really liked. The guests slowly started trickling in and by six, the house was full with friends and family. The wine and kababs flowed and so did the conversation.

Hope was the centre of attention, happily mingling with everyone and playing clown, irking Shanta Bai even more. She tripped over him and spilt a bowl of fruit punch. Sumit got home at seven to see the surprise of his life. We cut the cake together; he fed me a small piece and gave me a quick peck on my lips. 'Thank you sweetheart, this was totally unexpected. You've done a great job managing everything. Oh by the way, you look stunning in that dress.' I blushed and gave him a tight hug.

When dinner was laid and everyone had settled down, Sudha came up to me and gave me a bear hug. 'Pri, you look so good! I'm so happy to see you smiling again.' Watching Sudha hugging me didn't go down well with my jealous little Hope. He came bounding towards me, seeking my attention. I picked him up, patted him affectionately and got him his food bowl with a little piece of cake, which vanished in a flash of a second. He whimpered with those soft eyes asking for more. 'It looks like you've been starving the poor dog, Pri.' We both burst into peals of laughter, but Hope didn't seem to care, he was too busy licking the bowl for every last crumb of cake.

Sudha and I chatted for a long time and she filled me in on what had been happening in the fashion circuit. 'Suds, I think I want to design again,' I said.

'That's great Pri, you should. You should start from where you left off.'

'Yeah, I'll have to work from home for a while though. If I leave this little monster alone at home, he'll make sure the house looks like a cyclone just hit it,' I chuckled.

'Taking care of him is just like taking care of a baby, isn't it...' she bit her tongue as she realized what she'd just said. 'I'm sorry Pri, I didn't mean to upset you.'

'Don't worry about it Suds, I'm absolutely fine now,' I smiled. 'I have Hope,' I said looking down at him, and he looked right back at me. *Of course you do*, his eyes said.

The Right Thing to Do

PARITOSH UTTAM

I hadn't read the paper for days. I wasn't supposed to, until I reached the judgement—to avoid getting influenced by public opinion and all that blah—and I hadn't, because I take my duties seriously. So when I found a copy of today's *Times* on the side table, I gently prised off Roshni's arm from around my waist and picked up the paper. The only story it seemed to carry was the death sentence I had pronounced on the convicts.

Roshni stirred and dug her nails into my bare skin. 'Lie down,' she mumbled. When I didn't budge, she propped herself on an elbow and squinted in the light. 'What do they say?'

I snorted, and quoted from the paper: 'Capital punishment in this age indicates an uncivilised society, but Justice Ahluwalia does not think so.' 'The Punjab and Haryana High Court seems to believe in the barbaric adage of an eye for an eye.' 'These yellow, corrupt journalists!' I burst out.

Stroking my chest soothingly, Roshni baby-talked, 'Is Honourable Justice Ahluwalia angry?'

But I was far too enraged to be soothed so easily. 'As if molesting a young girl, mutilating and then strangling her is part of civilized society. As if the judgement of these khap panchayats is civilised. Do these people even deserve to live? If the Indian penal code allowed me, I would have the men buggered, castrated and then strangled. The noose is too good for them.'

'Good news?'

I glared at her. This was not the time for puns. On such occasions, I had a sharp suspicion that Roshni was playing the fool with me.

She could not be dumb; you don't become a practising lawyer in the High Court in your early thirties if you are dumb!

'You must be right,' she said, gently, trying to mollify me.

'Of course I am. It is the right thing to do.' I crushed the paper and flung it. 'I am the judge. I know what's fair and right. Don't people think of the victim and her family before sympathising with the murderer?'

Roshni's patient stroking gradually had its effect. I grew calmer.

I realised I was breathing too fast and it wasn't good for the heart.

Now she twirled my chest hair and the sensation was satisfying: it gave me the courage and confidence that I was right; I felt like a man. I glanced further down and I couldn't say I was dissatisfied by what I saw: it wasn't a sixty-year-old man's body. All it took was discipline—both mental and physical, to believe that even at sixty, you had quite a life ahead of you. And it wasn't just my vanity telling me so; Roshni's presence in my life was proof enough that I was right.

'It's about honour, Roshni. When one doesn't have honour, one does immoral, unethical deeds, even when one's conscience protests. Look at today's politicians. By rights, they ought to be the upholders of our ideals. But in reality they are synonyms for avarice, corruption, hypocrisy, and everything that's dishonourable.'

Roshni giggled. 'I love it when you talk big words. Tussi vocabulary bari changi hai.'

I patted her cheek. Again, she was playing. 'Come on, you are a lawyer.' I said.

'Reading those words in big fat books are fine. But when you use them in your speech, so naturally...that's what I like about you.'

'That's all?' I asked, a little hurt.

'And of course...' Roshni's downward glance completed her answer.

My feelings assuaged, I continued where I had left off. 'We used to have leaders like Lal Bahadur Shastri who resigned taking moral responsibility when a train accident occurred. Can you imagine that happening today? Now our leaders aren't merely thick-skinned; they have bulletproof hides.'

I knew I was boring her as she tried to stifle a yawn, but I was in this post-coital philosophical mood that I didn't want to disturb.

'Today, if someone says, "You think you are Gandhi?", he is not complimenting, he is mocking you. What a fall, what a tragedy! Becoming a Gandhi today is foolishness of the highest order. Your only place is in museums and history textbooks, not in the real, living world.'

My discourse was acting like a soporific to her. She kept nodding and falling forward, and yet I carried on.

'Honour, justice, fair play, morals, ethics, duty, responsibility... meaningless words that ought to be struck off from the dictionary. Archaic and obsolete nonsense. Honour killing? What an oxymoron! What honour is there in killing?'

My mobile piped the alarm I had set for 4.00 p.m. I struggled out of bed and began pulling on my trousers. Roshni looked upset.

'I have to drop my daughter to the station. She's going back to her college in Delhi.'

'Can't your wife drop her, instead?' she pouted.

'She can't drive. Besides,' I said, buttoning up my shirt, 'it's a man's job. It's my duty as her father.'

She watched me tuck in my shirt, zip up and fasten my belt. 'It's the right thing for you to do?' she asked.

'It's the right thing for me to do.' I took in her supine form, and suddenly overcome by the sight of her vulnerability and her loveliness—the rise of her breasts tantalisingly covered by the sheet—rushed over and kissed her. 'I will be back soon.'

'Word of honour?' she asked.

'Word of honour.' I said. But again, I had the nagging suspicion that she was playing with me.

•◆

Liberation

MALATHI JAIKUMAR

Chamundi would never know the Thank God Its Friday feeling or even what TGIF meant. Not only because she did not know English but also because she did not like Fridays. And she did not like Fridays because she dreaded Saturday evenings.

That was when her husband would stagger home drunk and pick a quarrel with her for the flimsiest of reasons. In the small two-roomed hutment, her two children would pretend to be asleep in the next room, for no child could really, truly sleep in the middle of all the noise and shouting. After cursing and throwing things around he would pick up his weapon. A very thin, smooth, twig like stick that tapered very gradually, to a fine, almost whip-like end. He would caress the stick for a while and then curl his thick fingers over the flat polished end. He aimed unerringly at her ankles and the thin end of the stick would come stinging like a red-hot wire. He was careful not to strike her on her arms or face. Only on her ankles or below the knees.

Initially the sari took part of the beating but when she found her sari being torn to shreds she hitched it up and took the beating on her legs. She did not have the money for more saris. Better to have scarred legs that could be covered up by a sari than to have no sari at all.

At first she tried not to cry but whimpered when she could bear it no longer. Her whimpering would turn him on and he would then cast the stick aside and take her forcefully. Now she began whimpering and moaning earlier to hasten the end. She knew peace would reign only when he was satisfied and fell asleep almost instantly.

Then her ten-year-old son would creep out silently. He would wet a piece of soft cloth with water from the matka and press it against the livid welts and bruised skin. It felt cool and soothing and she would hug him gratefully and limp over to the other room, glad that another Saturday was behind her and that now she had six days to heal. She would drift off to a fitful sleep, sandwiched between her son and her six-year-old daughter.

It had not always been like this. She remembered her life in the village, the sugar cane fields, the pond where she had played with her friends for hours together, climbing up mango trees for a stolen treat and the sheer, unbridled joy of being young. That lasted till her fourteenth birthday after which the restrictions began.

She had to stay at home, wear a mellakku over her paavadai and blouse to preserve her modesty and not talk to the men folk unless it was necessary and even then to keep her eyes downcast. She was very pretty and at fifteen she was married to the boy who worked as a handy man. He had an aptitude for repairing or setting right everything, from an ordinary cycle to the two or three tractors in the village owned by the more affluent farmers.

He was a strapping lad, dark and well-built and Chamundi, like all the girls in the village, bowed to the wishes of the elders when they proposed marriage. Her first son was born even before they had completed one year of marriage and the second, a girl followed after four years.

Her husband always had a restless streak in him and often spoke of moving out of the village to the city where he said he could make much more money with his skills. He could even learn how to repair cars and maybe one day he could even buy a car. When his dreams were mocked at, he stopped speaking about it but continued to nurture it in his heart. One day a group of five—three men and two women—arrived as volunteers for educating the villagers on hygiene, sanitation and family planning. The sight of their shiny cars, the sleek cell phones and laptops, their modern clothes, their smart talk and confidence rekindled and stoked the fires of restlessness.

With renewed determination he followed the visitors around for a week and before they left he managed to get a name and address in the city where he could go to look for a job.

Within a month he was in the city, got a job in a factory and three months later brought his wife and children there. For Chamundi it marked the beginning of living in a cramped room, sharing squalid toilets and fighting for water. The village had been primitive too but it was clean and she did not have to worry about the children roaming around freely. In the city there was no one she could trust. She heard horror tales of kidnappings and maiming of children and dared not let the little ones out of sight for long. She felt bad to keep them cooped up but fretted herself sick when they were away.

She was also unnerved by the vastness of the city. She felt like a little speck of a star in an ever-expanding universe. Poverty in the village did not divest a person of pride but poverty in the city seemed to degrade the soul. It turned the division between the haves and the have-nots into a great chasm, while the glitter and the glamour that beckoned just a stone's throw away from the dingy dwellings made one yearn for luxuries that were totally unnecessary and unsuitable.

Two years later, he got a promotion and they moved to the present two-room tenement that had a small bathroom that made all the difference. The factory paid him enough to live comfortably. He would bring her flowers once a week and three saris a year, one each for Deepavali, Pongal and the Tamil New Year. He played with the children and bought them milk barfis and toys now and then.

He had always been a great devotee of Balaji and had a huge picture of the deity as seen in Tirupathi. It was an almost life-size painting on cloth and had been given to him by a wealthy client as reward for helping to deliver a rather large order in a very short time. Every detail of the ornate jewels that adorned the crown, hands, feet and body was etched in gold paint and the flowers, especially the rose petals, looked very real. The painting of the gleaming black deity surrounded by shimmering gold lamps dominated the small room.

He would stand before it every morning and pray with his head bowed. His grandmother had been a great devotee he said and Balaji would appear in her dreams and talk to her and foretell major events in the family. His mother had told him that the old woman had known about the child quickening in her womb even before she knew it herself. The grandmother, prompted by Balaji, had predicted the birth of her first grandson. This made him feel unique—almost as if his birth had been ordained by God for a special reason.

When their daughter was four years old he was caught red-handed, stealing from the factory store house. He was suspended immediately and the investigation revealed that he had been pilfering expensive spare parts steadily over the past year. He lost his job without any termination benefits whatsoever. His meagre savings disappeared in the next few months. He would get one job after another but it never lasted for more than a few weeks, sometimes even less. Chamundi never knew when he was hired or fired. He would leave home in the morning and return at night and she could smell liquor on his breath. She wondered where he got the money for his drinks. One by one their joys vanished. No flowers, no saris and no sweets for the children. Even one meal a day was a blessing. He became morose and silent as he drifted from one odd job to another. The only thing that did not change was his prayers to Balaji morning and evening.

Then finally, one day he landed a job—a job that he did not talk about. Chamundi was sure it was something shady for all her efforts to glean some information from him proved futile. He left for work in the evening and returned early in the morning and slept till way past lunch time. Night shift he said. He acquired a cell phone and would start receiving calls from late afternoon till he left for work.

Money flowed in again along with the chocolates, flowers and occasional saris. But that was also when he began to drink heavily every Saturday. The beatings started a year later. And continued every week.

He still worshipped the picture of Balaji but he had moved it to the other room so that he could drink and beat her without the deity looking down at him. Chamundi had resigned to her fate. She hoped someday he would tire of his routine and go elsewhere to seek his pleasure. Some women she knew were happy when their husbands went to other women. Now she knew why.

One Friday evening he came home early packed a few clothes and went away. He had some work in another city, he said and he would be back in a week.

Chamundi went delirious with delight. The children, infected by her gaiety, pranced around and soon all three were playing boisterously. She decided she would take the children to the fair ground and then visit the temple on the outskirts of the city. She had some money saved up and hidden under her clothes. It was just about enough money to buy them something good to eat and maybe take a ride on the giant wheel. It could stretch to buying some trinkets for herself she thought and maybe even a toy for her son and a little doll for her daughter.

For the first time in years she looked forward to Saturday. She woke up early, washed her long, black hair and plaited it, letting it hang snakelike down her back. She wore the brightest sari she had and all the glass bangles she could find so that they jangled merrily with each movement of her hand. The children needed no coaxing. They were up and raring to go, excitedly plying her with questions.

The ride on the bus, looking out of the window, munching warm roasted peanuts, playing little games with the children and answering their endless questions would be etched in her mind forever. She would remember the smells, sights, the colour of the clothes they wore, the sunlight and every little detail of the trip very vividly for as long as she was alive. The hours flew by in a blur of giantwheels; shrieks of delight; pink candy floss; row upon row of little shops; gaudy, printed shirts and shiny synthetic saris; ribbons fluttering like multicoloured butterflies; bangles and earrings winking seductively in the sunlight and an overpowering smell of food, chutneys, fried bhajjis, sweets and flowers. She gorged herself on the bhajjis licking the tangy chutney off her fingers.

They made their way to the temple after the fair. It was nearly six by the time they reached the Mariamman temple on the outskirts of the town. It was already crowded and she had to push her way to the front dragging her children with her. She managed to get a little space on a step near a pillar. She could see the deity, a voluptuous figure in gleaming black stone, clad in a chilly red sari with a green and gold border that shimmered in the light of the oil lamps. The sculpture was bedecked with jewels, the earrings and the nose ring dazzling brilliantly in the dark room. The fragrance of oil, camphor, burning wicks, fruits and flowers mingled with the odour of sweat, cheap perfumes and lotions suffused the air, making her slightly nauseous.

Some space had been cleared in the middle of the crowd and stout ropes cordoned off the area. People pushed and jostled, straining against the ropes. A group of men and women began singing Mariamman songs to the accompaniment of a couple of drums and bells.

Chamundi turned to the middle-aged woman standing next to her.

'What's happening?' she asked.

'Have you never been here before?' came the reply. 'Why today is the final day of the three-day festival and there are two women here who will go into a trance. Mariamma comes to them and speaks to us through them.'

Chamundi had heard of women getting into a trance and had always wondered how much of it was real and how much was faked.

But the moment the thought entered her head she would chide herself for doubting people's devotion to the goddess. Today she was excited that she would be able to see it all and judge for herself.

It grew more hot and humid. The beating of the drums and the bells grew louder. The Mariamman songs acquired a renewed urgency and passion. Many of the spectators and devotees began to clap their hands and sing along.

Two women with garlands around their necks moved forward.

One was a stout, dark woman with salt and pepper hair,

well-oiled and pulled back in a tight coil at the nape of her neck. She was probably in her mid-fifties. The other was a much younger woman, with shapely breasts and slim hips, her figure accentuated by the sari tucked in at her waist.

They had been singing along with the crowd and gradually stepped forward into the clearing in the middle. They danced, swaying gently to the music their eyes half-closed. They moved around languidly, both of them immersed in their individual and completely different worlds, impervious to all the noise and crowd. They reminded Chamundi of rag dolls with hands and head flopping around. The crowd was hypnotized, their eyes never leaving the two figures moving back and forth without a pause.

All of a sudden the crowd let out a collective gasp as the older woman came to a halt, straight and stiff as if she had been pulled up like a puppet on a string. The younger woman continued to gyrate completely oblivious of her partner. Gradually her movements grew faster.

The stout woman slid down on her knees and sank slowly to the floor to sit on her heels, her head rolling round and round till Chamundi feared she would break her neck. The children clung to her; their eyes round with excitement tinged with fear. By now the younger woman had become rigid, drawing herself up to her full height. Her loose plait had come undone and her hair was all over her shoulders and face. The sari had slipped exposing the curve of her breasts under the tight blouse. Her eyes were wide open and she mumbled something in a low guttural tone.

The crowd went into frenzy, chanting and clapping faster and faster. A man in an orange dhoti lit some camphor and walked around the women. Shouts of 'Amma' and 'Mariamma' rent the air as men and women in the crowd got caught up in the excitement. Some cautiously inched forward, each one shouting a question, at first tentatively, then with more confidence, and then more authoritatively. People pushed and jostled with growing vigour till the air was full of voices. The younger woman was now crouching on the ground, twisting and turning at the waist, at times swaying in a full circle. Her hair streamed out all around her, even covering her face.

'Mariamma, will my daughter get married this year?'; 'Amma, cure my son'; 'Mariamma, give me a grandson'; 'Bless me Amma, bless me'; 'Bring my husband back to me'; all blended together in one great roar. The two women were now totally possessed. They swayed back and forth, slapped the ground with their hands and made weird moaning noises that the crowd interpreted as answers to their questions.

More camphor was lit. The incense sticks and the lumps of sambrani on red-hot cluster of coal filled the air with fragrant smoke. The bells began to ring. The two women were still in a trance but their movements gradually became slower. The younger woman was drenched with sweat, her clothes clinging to her youthful body, her clear dark skin glistening in the light of the lamps. The older woman fell in a swoon and minutes later the younger one also fell in a faint. People left some fruits and flowers by their side as offerings. Some bowed and touched their feet. Some threw coins or flowers.

Long after she had reached home and put the weary children to bed, Chamundi was haunted by the sight of the women and continued to think about it the whole week. While the children revelled in the absence of their father, Chamundi was more subdued and silent. Her mind was full of questions. What was the spirit or power that possessed these women? Did it come from outside or did they have it within them, dormant till roused on a certain day? Whatever it was she could see that no person could resist being awed by the 'performance'. She had seen that even the more menacing of men in the crowd had gaped in wonder and had touched the feet of the women after they swooned. They could be brutes but they were afraid of the unknown, wary of something they could not understand or explain.

Her husband returned late on Friday looking tired. He had bought some clothes for the children and a box of sweets. He was quite pleasant and did not seem very curious about what they had done while he was away. Perhaps he is conserving his energy for tomorrow thought Chamundi wryly.

The next day she was ready for him. She cooked his favourite fish curry and rice and practiced her moves in her mind. By the time he staggered home the children were in bed. Her daughter was fast asleep, but she knew her son would be awake. She anticipated her husband's every need and tried her very best not to give him a chance to pick a fight. She served dinner, sitting beside him, fanning him and watched him eat with relish.

It was while he was having his second helping that she let the fan drop from her limp hand. At the same time her eyes became half-closed and she began swaying gently.

'What's wrong with you woman?' he shouted but made no move to come closer.

She began to move from the waist in a circular motion, rolling her head at the same time. She could feel her hair swing around. She slowly stood up, her hands rigid and stiff by her side.

'Stop this right now or I will thrash you,' he shouted. Chamundi's heart sank. If he did not believe her it could become much worse. She began to mumble indistinctly as she swayed from side to side. She tried to recall every movement of the two women at the temple. Very gradually she changed her voice and began to speak in a low, male voice. Very slowly, dragging out every word she repeated over and over again. 'I have come to bless you.' At first her voice was so low he could hardly hear or understand her.

Through her half-closed eyes she could see him looking a bit confused. He did not want to displease his Lord and yet he could not bring himself to believe his eyes. There was a touch of fear mixed with suspicion in his glance. This was the crucial moment. She pulled herself up to her full five feet three frame, opened her eyes as wide as she could, flared her nostrils and compressed her lips. She knew the effect would be quite startling because she had practiced it in front of the mirror.

'I have come to bless you. Bring me the aarati,' she continued in her guttural tone. Her glance was now fixed six inches above his head and as she spoke she started rolling her eyes. She lurched closer to him and saw him move back startled. She saw her son creep out of bed and stand clutching the door. His eyes were round with surprise as he gazed at his mother who seemed to have been transformed into another person altogether. 'I am pleased. I will bless you.'

Her movements became more rapid and she was now lost in a world of her own. She found that as she psyched herself to go into a trance she almost convinced herself that she truly was in a trance. This is what people felt like when they acted she thought. If you put yourself in a role, body and soul, gradually the role took over the person. She began to enjoy herself. She loved the swaying of her head and the feel of her hair on her face. Her body seemed to have a will of its own and she marvelled at her own movements that were almost inspired. She felt powerful because for the first time she had instilled fear in him. It was a heady feeling.

He stood transfixed. His right hand, as yet unwashed and held away from his body, still had traces of the rice and fish curry. He could not move or speak.

'Bring me the aarati. I will bless you.' Her voice now became more insistent. 'Bring aarati. Bring aarati,' she kept mumbling.

Suddenly, galvanized into action he ran and washed his hands, then went into the next room and came back with the camphor and the brass holder. He quickly struck a match and set the camphor alight. 'Govinda, Govinda,' he chanted, waving the camphor up and down in front of her. The light from the flame cast an eerie glow on her features. She almost sneezed when the smoke came straight into her face but managed to stifle it.

She continued to sway and kept repeating 'Bless you. Bless you,' till she slowly sank to the floor in a stupor. He put the aarati down and stood looking down at her. It was a good fifteen minutes before she opened her eyes and moved her limbs heavily, as if she was coming out of a deep sleep.

He came to her side and bent low peering into her face.

'What happened? Did I faint? I feel so tired. My head aches,' she mumbled.

'Don't you remember anything?' he asked.

'No I just feel sore all over,' she said.

'Don't worry. You just rest for now. Balaji's blessing is with us. He spoke to me through you. Just sleep and regain your strength. He might come again.'

Her son took her hand and led her to the bed. Settling herself between the two children she turned to wink at her son and saw him bury a smile in his pillow.

He did not stop drinking but the weekly beatings did. Once in a while just to remind him she would go into a trance. He never touched her again. He probably went to other women but that did not bother her. She was happy enough to be left alone. Uneducated, illiterate and economically dependent, Chamundi had liberated herself in her own way.

·◆

Notes of Discord

PARITOSH UTTAM

The funny part was that—no, it was not funny, no matter whose point of view you looked from—rather, the irony was that it was Jai who had suggested cleaning up his study. At the threshold, leaving for another of his frequent week-long business tours to the US, he had made a sarcastic remark that if he had free time on his hands, the house would look a lot less chaotic.

Meera, who took pride in the way she maintained her household, was stung. Jai saw her hurt and tried to make it up with an overtly affectionate hug and a kiss. 'Tell you what, Meera, why don't you plan that Maldives trip we have been putting off?'

She accepted that as his way of apology—if, after four years of marriage, you did not consider such minor quarrels as an integral part and parcel of life, you needed a reality check. So as soon as Jai left for the airport, she went into his study because she knew it was that room he had had in mind.

She had been wary all along of disturbing his books and documents for fear of mixing them up and upsetting him. How was she to know he expected her to sort out this room too? When he returned she would present him a transformed study room, with neatly arranged shelves and cabinets for all his material: management books here, fiction there; files and folders in that cabinet, his diaries, over there…

In terms of calendar pages, Meera's joy on discovering Jai's diary lasted exactly six months: 1 July to 31 December. She had no inkling that Jai maintained a personal diary. For two doubtful seconds, she wondered if it was ethical of her to read it. But how ethical was it of him to not even let her know that he kept one? By the clock, it took her fifteen minutes of flipping the diary to realise that all the endearing observations she read were not those of a doting husband about his wife. The simile about a stomach as flat as an LCD TV screen could not possibly refer to her.

For once, Meera was relieved that Jai was away on tour. That was the only positive; the rest of her feelings were varying degrees of disbelief, jealousy and hurt. One line that drove a nail through her heart was: 'M2 is gentle and caring'. A sultry seductress enticing her husband she could try to comprehend, but another woman surpassing her in caring and warmth?

Her overwhelming awareness, however, was of her gullibility.

For how long? The diary she had discovered was last year's. She could not find another diary either preceding the one in her hands, or carrying on where it stopped. Had Jai stopped writing because the affair had ended, or just because he had run out of pages in that diary? And why start in the middle? Even after poring over each entry with masochistic detail, she couldn't figure a start or an end to this M2. Did he actually want to her to find this diary, and hence the casually dropped hint about clearing the study? Or had he simply become careless?

Maybe it had all started years ago, before Amit's birth, or even before she met and married Jai. But in that case she would be M2, not M1. Meera heard her own ghastly laughter: in her husband's mind she was only to be distinguished based on a numeric suffix.

Perhaps it began when she was carrying, shapeless and irritable, while thinking of Jai as the most wonderful husband catering to her every whim. Meera felt ashamed of being consoled because the diary references to her were pitying, and not derogatory. 'Poor M1 has no idea; so satisfied with her conventional life.' 'Leaving M1 for M2 is tempting but impractical. There's Amit.'

For her, there were other factors to consider, besides Amit. Like relinquishing the security and status the pay-packet of a top-notch IT manager in an MNC in Bangalore secured; scouring the rust off her own long-disused skills to make herself employable again; the pain of explaining to everyone and their aunt why her marriage had come apart at the seams. Walking out of marriage was not like walking out of a shop because you thought you were getting a bad deal.

Her most galling thought was that had it not been for the diary, her world would still be intact; Jai would be the perfect husband; she would be busy planning their luxury cruise to Maldives in the summer. Couldn't she simply pretend she had never discovered the diary, and everything could go back to being how it was? Jai had no plans of abandoning her or her conventionality, regardless of the scorn he heaped on it.

All Meera decided to do, was to start keeping her own diary. She found an unused diary of the previous year—there were plenty, presented by Jai's office or by other acquaintances, still lying gift-wrapped—and imagined what to write.

'J away on tour. A in nursery. Bored. Called P over again. So good to feel a strong, manly chest for a change.'

Whenever Jai discovered her diary, as she would ensure he did, it should burn him up. Meera got busy filling up the pages. She had only a week to re-create one whole year.

It's a Small World

AHMED FAIYAZ

Rahul's Apartment, Pali Hill, Bandra

Rahul moved towards Kajal who was fussing with the pillows on the couch, and ran his fingers through her tresses. 'You look stunning! Don't worry love; it's all going to go well tonight. My friends are going to love you.' Kajal sat back looking nervous; she was all decked up in a Zara party dress while Rahul looked dapper in his black Ralph Lauren shirt and Diesel Jeans. He had just managed to get home in time to get changed. So Kajal had supervised all the preparations for their first dinner party together as a couple. She was slowly beginning to find her feet in Mumbai, and in his apartment, having moved in a week ago.

She was from London, and they had met in Rome, where both of them had spent a month learning photography together. The attraction had been instantaneous with the two plunging into a relationship within a few days of meeting. They'd been the only Indians in a group of eight and though they were from different backgrounds—she was a freelance graphic designer, the daughter of a leading surgeon in London, and he was from a leading business family, and ran a lounge in Bombay called Leap Over, with a school friend— they'd hit it off over a common love for spectacular Baroque architecture. They spent a whole day together, during their first weekend in Rome, taking pictures of the St Peters Basilica, Pantheon and the Colosseum.

'You think? You've grown up with these people. Aren't they going to judge me? I mean we dated for just a month before you proposed. I moved in with you last week. They might think it's a little too soon, yeah?' She was different from them, she sounded different, having had a British upbringing, in an English neighbourhood.

'Chill, they have their own issues in life. They're happy for me. I've told them so much about you.' She looked sceptical, 'Trust me babe, they're looking forward to seeing you.' His sudden decision to marry Kajal had shocked his friends, but they were pleased for him at the same time.

'Tell me about this situation again. Sohail, your business partner, and Karishma used to date right? And then her folks got her married off to this Akhil.'

'Yes, that's right; they were so into each other. Neither of them could convince their parents to accept them. The whole Hindu-Muslim thing took a toll on their relationship. Imagine! They'd been together since school and stuck it through college. They were the serious couple in our gang. Life's got its own agenda I guess. I don't believe these two have even met since Karishma got married a year back. I catch up with them separately. Akhil doesn't make it easier; he's quite stiff and difficult with her. But yeah, I somehow persuaded them to come here.'

'That's good, hopefully they've both moved on. It'll take some attention off me, for sure!'

'Ha ha, yes,' he kissed her on the nose, 'How do the enchiladas look?'

'They look yummy. You're right, Charley's down the road makes some great food. It was a good decision to give them a catering order.' 'Yeah, like I keep saying, I'm always right.' The doorbell went before Kajal could retort.

Kajal opened the door to Sohail who walked in and hugged her.

'So we finally meet, you're beautiful,' he said. Sohail handed the bottle of wine he had picked up, noticing that Kajal looked gorgeous in her sexy black dress. She came across as someone who was smart and intelligent as well. He smiled at his best friend, sitting across the room, and gave him a nod of approval.

The boys poured a glass of wine for themselves and spoke about Rahul's recent trip to London.

'My in-laws to be have a place in the country. It's beautiful, dude!' Rahul said with enthusiasm, 'We should evaluate the opportunity of doing something there. My future father-in-law can facilitate things; he knows people...'

'... who know people?' Sohail said with a wink at Kajal. She grinned back at him, feeling comfortable with his uncomplicated acceptance of her place in Rahul's life.

'So when's the D-day, guys?'

'Even though I proposed in London and Kajal accepted, my parents want to have a formal engagement party. The engagement is at Four Seasons as I may have told you. My parents are inviting all their famous and wealthy friends. Not my ideal scene but I'm letting it pass for mum and dad's sake.' Rahul grimaced, 'For the wedding we'll keep it small. Hopefully, we can get away with a small private ceremony at your new hotel in Lavasa. It will be perfect, just family and friends—mine can stay at our holiday home, and hers could stay over at the rooms at the resort,' he added, very much an involved groom.

'That's great dude, you let me know and I'll set it up.' He turned to Kajal and gestured towards her empty hands, 'Let me pour you a glass of wine. My boy is not treating you right! You've finally belled the most eligible of Pali Hill. But tell me how do you like Mumbai so far?'

'Overwhelming and crowded,' she said with a slight smile. 'I like the neighbourhood though, and I quite like the weather; its grey and depressing in London right now. So all in all it's not so bad, I reckon. I've been bonding with his family.' Kajal wondered if her decision to marry Rahul was taken in haste. After all, he had spoken to her of many dalliances in the past. Her friends wanted her to wait and not put all her trust in him, in a hurry.

'Yeah, that's critical, claw your way into the blue-blooded Mehta clan.' He took a sip, with a wry grin on his face, while Kajal nodded along with a polite smile, still lost in her thoughts.

'Dude, they aren't so bad. I live separately anyway, so Kajal has her space,' he said, patting her on her thigh as she finished her glass of wine. They heard the doorbell again, and Kajal went to see who it was.

Karishma walked in with Akhil who seemed like a friendly guy. Both of them greeted her cheerfully, and offered her congratulations. Karishma hugged Rahul and Kajal affectionately. 'The ring looks even more beautiful on your finger,' she said to Kajal with a glitter in her eyes, while Akhil sized up Sohail, who remained seated and poured himself another glass of wine. He said a terse hello to the couple, and began a conversation with Kajal who sat next to him.

The mood for the evening was calm and relaxed, though there were undercurrents of tension between Karishma and Sohail, while songs from *Elements*, Mike Oldfield's famed album played in the background. He still pined for Karishma, but she had systematically cut him out of her life. Akhil, a real estate contractor, made conversation about the projects he had recently completed. He heard out Rahul talking excitedly about their upcoming lounge in Gurgaon, and how some of his other investments were doing.

Karishma and Sohail gazed at each other from time to time. They tried to avoid talking to each other by encouraging Kajal to talk, asking her about her work and life in London. The group then moved across to the dining table to enjoy a scrumptious meal, which was followed by delectable mango and blueberry cheese cake ordered from a chain of recently set up pastry shops that Rahul's company had invested in.

The wine flowed and Akhil and Sohail eased up enough to laugh at each other's jokes. Sohail spoke about his advisory work with a microfinance company to support and boost their programmes, while Rahul was supporting his mother's charity, which involved the building of thirty primary schools in Maharashtra. Akhil nodded along with scepticism not really buying into their approach to life. He asked them cautiously if they knew of any property for redevelopment.

'It's great having you guys over tonight. Unfortunately, Rohan is away in Hong Kong, and I sure am missing Nikhil and Dipti.'

'I don't think Nikhil is missing us,' Sohail said with a grin. The rest of them shared a laugh recalling Nikhil's pursuit of Dipti for five years before finally getting her to tie the knot.

Kajal looking distracted asked Akhil, 'Have we met before? You look so familiar. I can't remember when and where; it's going to drive me mad now, trying to place you!' Rahul sitting next to her gave her an absent-minded kiss on the cheek as he continued reminiscing with his college friends.

'You must have seen me in London. I travelled to London a lot last year for a project I was working on.' Akhil said with a shrug, and yawned before pouring himself another glass of wine.

Kajal took a sip of her wine as she regarded Akhil, 'That's

unlikely. I was in Dubai till six months ago. I was posted there by my previous company.'

'I don't know, maybe someone like me? There are lots of Punjabis in London. Karishma and I also get featured in newspapers,' he said dismissively, 'We've had our pictures clicked at parties a number of times. If you read those kind of tabloids you could have seen us in them. I can't place you though. Sorry... I don't believe we've met before tonight.' Akhil turned his attention to Karishma effectively ending the discussion. Sohail and Rahul were having a conversation of their own about the Tata Group taking over a large automobile company in the UK. Kajal, looking confused, shifted her focus to serving more cheese cake to her guests.

They moved from the table and got comfortable on the couch.

Catching up in a group had really got the nostalgia going and Kajal sat back in the crook of Rahul's arm as he happily shared anecdotes about old friends and batch mates. One of the boys kept the wine glasses topped and a relaxed hour sped by. Kajal got up and dragged herself to the restroom. She'd had more than her usual limit of three glasses and felt a bit tipsy. 'Watch your step honey,' Rahul said watching her walk away.

In the restroom, she washed her face, and looked at herself in the mirror. A scene from eight months ago flashed in her memory.

Her group from college had gone to Greece for a weekend, and they had decided to enjoy the evening at Ibiza, the resort's popular discotheque by the beach. She remembered a friend of hers from school—Sharmishta Sen Gupta—had called out to her from across the dance floor. Kajal immediately remembered where she had first met Akhil. She got out of the restroom and called out to Rahul, 'Could you please come to the bedroom for a minute?' she said worriedly.

'Can't it wait sweetheart? We have guests, remember?' he

shouted back, and she heard peals of laughter in the living room. 'Alright, I'm coming in a minute,' he added getting up.

Rahul walked into the room, and was startled by the expression on Kajal's face. This doesn't look good, he thought. They sat down on the bed and Kajal began to tell him what she remembered. As Kajal began relating the scene from the night in Ibiza, explaining how Akhil held Sharmishta close and danced through the night.

'Sharmishta worked in an advertising agency in London and was in Greece with her boyfriend, whom she introduced as a leading builder. Sharmishta had been pleased as punch as she told me that he planned the trip to bring in her birthday.' Listening to her, Rahul began getting angry.

Karishma and Akhil had moved to Rahul's balcony with their drinks, to enjoy the view of the promenade and the sea from his apartment. Rahul came out, and asked Sohail who was busy on his Blackberry to join him for a minute. Sohail followed him in and sat back looking furious as Rahul kept talking.

The three of them came back to the living room and signalled to Karishma and Akhil to come and sit down with them. 'We have something important that needs to be talked about,' Rahul told Akhil firmly. Sohail tried to calm down and seemed to be restraining himself with great difficulty. Karishma looked confused with the change in mood but instinctively leaned in to Kajal's hand on her arm.

Akhil snickered at the guys. 'What are you boys planning to do now; build a school to teach graphic design to the poor, headed by Kajal?' He had often joked to Karishma that emotion had no place in business and that he didn't believe in these visions of wanting to change the world and make it a better place. Sohail and Rahul exchanged glances, not looking amused, and only Karishma managed a faint smile.

'Sit down Akhil,' Sohail said, directing him to a seat positioned between him and Rahul, while Kajal took Karishma by her arm and made her sit on the couch next to her.

'Do you know a Sharmishta Sen Gupta? Does it ring a bell?' Rahul asked.

'What kind of a question is that?' Akhil said looking instantly agitated, 'I don't remember! What is it with you guys? I think we must leave. We have a number of things that we are busy with.'

Rahul in a cool but firm voice asked him, 'Well it's a pretty straight question. Do you know this girl and if you do, what is your relationship with her?'

'I'm not sure. What do you mean by asking me what my relationship with her is?' Akhil looked indignant and leaned in.

'Let's cut the chase man, I have no time for your lies and games,' Rahul said in a raised voice.

'I think I met a friend's friend in London with a name that sounds similar.'

'Spell it out,' Rahul said waving his arms.

'She's just a friend's friend in London, and we've partied together a few times. Can we leave, Karishma? It's quite late,' Akhil replied, and looked at her with urgency, wanting to get up and leave. His face began to lose its arrogance, and air of superiority, and he began to get fidgety, scratching his French beard. Karishma sat there ignoring him. Whatever this was about, she wanted to hear it.

Looking at Kajal and then at Sohail, Rahul said, 'Is she? Tell me then, why does she have a picture of you and her together framed up in her house? Strange isn't it! It's even stranger for her to claim that both of you are seeing each other for the last six months. It also baffles me that Sharmishta believes that your marriage to Karishma was forced and one you cannot break for the sake of your parents.'

Akhil looked away, trying to search for an answer. He stared at the ground unable to meet Karishma's eyes.

'Sharmishta or Mishti as she is popularly known happened to go to school with Kajal in London.' Rahul continued, which brought a look of horror on Akhil's face, and Karishma looked like she was going to cry. 'Kajal dropped by Mishti's place a few months ago and saw that pictures of the both of you adorn her walls. You also apparently bumped into Kajal with Mishti at Ibiza in Greece, a few months ago, where you were briefly introduced.'

Looking at Karishma, Sohail said, 'This Mishti is into advertising. She moved from London to Mumbai last month,' Sohail's tone turned hard as he pinned his gaze on Akhil, 'You might as well admit it. There isn't a point denying anything. We know what this girl does, and where she lives, so we can bring her in or go over to her place and see some of these interesting pictures.'

Akhil hesitated, and turned aggressively towards Sohail, looking at him with eyes filled with rage. 'You're the one conspiring against me; making a big deal about a girl I once used to date. You can't deal with Karishma and me being together. You can't stand the fact that she married me and not you. Stop conspiring against us and leave me alone. Karishma is with me now.'

Rahul interrupted him, 'Akhil cut it out. This isn't about Sohail and Karishma. This is about you. You can deny it but Kajal just spoke to Sharmishta and we could go over to her place and sort this out once and for all, but then you better be prepared to face the consequences. I try to be a nice guy to the extent I can but don't test my limits.'

Shifting his gaze away from Sohail, to the painting on the wall Akhil said, 'It's true. But it doesn't mean anything. I have feelings for you and I've been trying to end it anyway. She's a friend's friend from London, and got in touch with me when I went there to work on projects.' Karishma who had turned pale and was frozen in shock suddenly seemed to snap at the trite words. She took a step forward and tossed her glass of water into his face, 'How could you? How dare you?' she shrieked hysterically, as Kajal tried to calm her down. 'This is it, I can't believe that you would do this!' she said looking at him with anguish in her eyes.

'Karishma, I...listen to me. Let's go home and talk. I made a mistake, we can work this out,' he pleaded wiping his face with the sleeve of his designer cashmere sweater.

'Leave me alone Akhil! Please pack your bags and leave the apartment! My dad and my lawyer will get in touch with you. I can't believe you think we can work this out. I don't want to see your face!'

'You can't just throw me out; Calm down and stop shouting at me in front of your friends. Let's go home,' he said pulling her hand. 'Don't you dare bully her!' Sohail said enraged. He stepped in front of Akhil and gently moved Karishma behind him. He stood face to face with his nemesis. 'Get out of here Akhil. Otherwise believe me you won't have legs to stand on.'

'I suggest you pack your bags and leave. Karishma's family will take the next steps as necessary. You have the rest of the night to pick up what you need and leave,' Rahul added pointing his finger at Akhil.

Akhil attempted a brave stance, 'You can't tell me what to do! This is between Karishma and me and I am not leaving my home. It's between a husband and wife and has nothing to do with you.'

Rahul folded up his sleeves, 'Don't test me on what I can and cannot do. You son of a bitch, Karishma is like a sister. I'm not going to stand by and watch you hurt her. Leave.' Rahul inched forward no longer able to control his disgust. 'I told you not to go and get hitched to some bloke you barely know. I told you about his reputation, he used to hang out at my club for God's sake,' he said turning to Karishma.

Akhil took a step back and Sohail lunged at him. He grabbed Akhil by his collar, and pushed him against the wall. Before Akhil could react, he swung his fist at Akhil's jaw, and held him up against the wall, while Akhil looked at him with fear. Rahul and Kajal pulled him away, while Karishma stood there looking at them with an air of helplessness and misery.

I do not deserve this. What will people say? Oh, my life is ruined! My parents won't be able to look at people in the eye she realised. How will I face the world? What am I going to tell them?

Was I not good enough? People are going to laugh at me.

She saw Akhil lying in a heap on the floor, spitting out blood on Rahul's expensive Persian rug. Rahul pulled Sohail away. 'I can't believe you did this Akhil! Clean yourself up in the restroom downstairs, and get going. Karishma's lawyer or I will contact you soon,' Rahul said.

'Rahul! Sohail! Stop it! What have you done? It's for Akhil and me to sort this out,' she said with tears rolling down her cheek.

'Karishma….' Rahul walked up to her, and cupped her cheeks in his hands.

'No, Rahul, please, don't do this! I'm married to him,' she pleaded, as Akhil fumbled to get back on his feet. Sohail looked outraged. 'I need to talk to him and understand what happened. We need to sort this out.'

'Are you freaking….' Sohail moved closer to her, with his hands in the air.

'Sohail, please stay out of this. This is a family matter.' He looked at her, feeling stung. It was like she had slapped him. He shook with fury, turning his gaze from her to Rahul and then Kajal.

Akhil got up and walked towards the door. He looked at Kajal, his eyes filled with anger, having suffered the indignity of being abused and knocked about, and covered his mouth with one hand.

Karishma started to walk out behind him and then stopped in front of Sohail looking lost. Her hand almost reached out beseechingly. People will laugh at me. She snatched her hand back and walked out after her husband.

The three friends left behind were frozen in place. They seemed more betrayed than Karishma. Sohail had most likely broken a finger or two. Kajal went over to the pantry to find some ice cubes for his hand. Rahul consoled him, 'Well, at least we told her, like you wanted to. That damn son of a bitch!' and added, 'That was a nice hook dude! I should have got one in too.'

She came back holding a hand towel wrapped around ice-cubes, wondering how to put off the impending wedding…

•◆

Replay

PARITOSH UTTAM

It took Lata a few moments to realize the man was addressing her, and another few to understand that he was begging. He was dressed respectably enough, shirt and trousers intact, as respectable a man as she could expect on a suburban train in Mumbai.

'Just one hundred rupees, Ma'am. That's all I need to get back to Goa.'

Lata tried to relax by breathing deeper. Her one hand, she found, was clutching her purse and the other was at her throat, feeling for her necklace that she no longer wore. Why had the man singled her out in that jostling crowd?

'That's my home. Goa.'

That was something she had to learn quickly, to stay on guard.

Now that it had befallen her to be a part of this city of a teeming nineteen million, where people scurried like ants, living fifty thousand to a square mile and fighting for every breath, there was no other option. On guard on the streets against ruffians; in bazaars against unscrupulous shopkeepers; in the train against lecherous men deliberately bumping against women; and even at home against the suspicious knock on the door. But this man talking to her didn't appear to be a threat.

'This city, I tell you, Ma'am, is full of thieves. Yesterday my purse had five thousand rupees; today I don't have a purse. I just want to go home, away from here, away from lies and dishonesty.'

Wouldn't she, herself? What wouldn't she give to be far away from this frightening mass of people? The only one who seemed surprised by this man's speech was herself. The woman beside her, who had grudgingly vacated six inches of wooden seat for her, gazed vacantly out of the window at the speeding landscape. The rest either hid their eyes in their newspapers, or were simply busy maintaining their balance standing up in the swaying train. At least this kind of begging was a welcome change from the usual amputee thrusting his sawn off limb under your nose. And his English was surely better than that of certain people in her office.

'You think I am lying, don't you?' He was devoid of anger, his voice touched with resignation. 'I am a respectable man in my town. Do you think it is easy for me to beg in public? I appeal to you, Madam,' he said, his voice softening suddenly, 'because you looked like you could give someone a chance. You wouldn't be cynical like everybody else.'

So that made it the second appeal within two days to her trusting nature. Lata felt the edges of Vinod's email printout inside her purse. She didn't need to take it out, having read it four times since it had arrived the previous day. Why was only she expected to get over her distrust?

I know I don't deserve your forgiveness, Lata. I didn't value your love when I had it. But the shameless wretch that I am, I am back and hope for your forgiveness and love once more, but this time with the promise of never leaving your side.

He obviously did not remember that as one of their marriage

vows that he had already broken.

'Look Ma'am, give me your address and I will send the money back to you as soon as I get home. I give you my word.'

Now that the novelty of his fluent English was wearing off, his persistence was beginning to irritate. Lata felt flustered with the attention it was starting to get her. Despite their newspapers and vacant stares, everybody's ears were open. She fished inside her purse and got out a note.

'That's only fifty rupees, Ma'am.' 'I can't spare more.'

'But it won't be enough, Ma'am. You either trust someone or not; you cannot half-trust. I will send the money back. I swear.'

The longer she entertained him, the more embarrassing it was turning out. Her co-passengers had dropped their pretences and were looking on with unabashed curiosity. Lata handed over another note.

'Thank you so much. Your address?'

Lata began mumbling her address before realizing it was not a very intelligent thing to do in public. 'Forget it.'

'God will reward you for your kindness and trust,' the man said, edging away from her. At the next stop in Matunga, she saw him spring down the carriage and lose himself in the crowd in a matter of seconds.

As the train pulled away again with a shudder, the woman beside Lata spoke up. 'You shouldn't have given him the money. It's their daily business.'

Lata shrugged, forcing a casualness into her voice to mask her anger. 'Who knows? Maybe he was speaking the truth.' Why had she kept mum while the man was importuning her? 'Everybody deserves a chance,' Lata said. 'We need to trust people sometimes.'

'Not in Mumbai,' the woman said, barely able to keep the laughter out of her face.

'If only I had that much money to throw around,' someone sighed behind the cover of a newspaper.

Lata ignored them for the remainder of the journey. She was glad when the train reached CST and forced everyone to disembark. In the office, she couldn't wait for the day to end. During lunch break, she re-read Vinod's letter in a quiet moment.

Back home, after supper, Lata sat down to compose her reply on paper. She figured that in office she would not have the time to think what to write. When her colleagues would be away for lunch in the cafeteria, she could simply type out the letter in reply to Vinod's email. Two hours on, she found she had filled six pages detailing the anguish and rumble-tumble of emotions she had gone through after his abandoning her for another woman: the shock, the hurt, the insecurity, the humiliation, the practical business of having to earn her keep, but most of all, the terrifying loneliness.

Reviewing her own letter, Lata was seized by doubt. Maybe she was opening herself up too much, too quickly, to the same man who had betrayed her. She had to be more pragmatic this time around. In the second draft, she settled for a couple of lines, agreeing to meet him and talk things over. That would keep him from thinking she wasn't falling over herself getting back with him, though she was not sure she could maintain her poise when they met. Her heart thumped with a frightening intensity at the thought of meeting him again after so many months.

She was sure she was being stupid. How long must he have been cheating her, and yet at the same time, showering his affection on her, taking her to the movies, even helping her in the kitchen, without a quiver in his voice? She had been entirely bereft of suspicion and considered her arranged marriage so much better than those here-today-gone-tomorrow love and internet-based matches.

Vinod did not have a quiver in his voice even when he was calmly announcing that he could not stay any more with her, and while she frantically kept asking the same question—'But what did I do? Tell me, what did I do?'—she was so sure that the fault was hers.

He was sweet about that, very clear in his assertion that he was the culpable party. Of course the reason for this exceptional piece of honesty, she realized later, was his need of her cooperation in granting him a divorce by mutual consent.

But she could not half-trust. She kept both the drafts—the sentimental six-page one and the practical two-liner—in her purse, unable to decide which one to mail.

The letter-writing and her thoughts kept Lata awake late into the night. As a result, she woke up an hour later than usual and had to push the next day's schedule by an hour. But it was not much of a concern: her job as a process quality engineer in the IT department was not demanding. Her reaching work one day at eleven instead of ten wouldn't cause the skies to fall.

The day was bright and cheerful. Lata felt she was finally beginning to get used to Mumbai and its nuances: she thought the crowd in the 10.42 Fast to be different from the one in the 9.38 Fast. Given time, one probably could get used to anything— to loneliness, to crowds, to the jostling for every square inch of space, to squalor, to fancy skyscrapers standing tall amid clusters of slums.

'Just a hundred rupees, Ma'am. That's all I need to get back to my home in Goa.'

The man obviously did not recognize her. Perhaps it was hard to remember when you said the same thing to a gullible face in the crowd over and over, day after day. Lata felt her eyes smart with tears.

She opened her purse. The man faltered in his tale, disbelieving his easy success. Lata took out the letters, tore them, and let the wind snatch the pieces from her hand outside the train window.

•◆

The Biggest Problem

PARITOSH UTTAM

As soon as the old man woke up, he realized his situation was precarious. The growing pressure in the pit of his belly had disrupted his nap. Without a window in his side of the partition, it was as dark in the afternoon as it was at night. He was lucky, considering he had woken in time and not wet the bed, thus avoiding the hell his daughter-in-law would raise if the sheets had to be washed and hung to dry. But that also meant he couldn't wait much longer; he would have to go to the toilet soon. The cold only made the urge stronger.

But was she awake? He strained his ears to catch any sound of wakefulness from the other side of the partition—utensils clanging, water running, bed creaking—but heard nothing. His heart sank. His daughter-in-law was asleep.

She had forbidden him to cross her room while she had her afternoon nap. But was it his fault that the way to the toilet led through her room? The sliding door in the partition creaked and scraped, his shuffling across the room was noisy, and then the racket he created in the bathroom with bucket and mug, everything, she told her husband, destroyed her fleeting sleep. And of all the people in the house, if she didn't deserve an uninterrupted hour of sleep, then she didn't know who did, she declared in a voice she ensured was loud enough to carry over to him.

Sitting up in his creaking cot, the old man groped for his slippers on the ground with his feet. Was it his fault that the house was full of sounds? His cot creaked, the partition door creaked, the floorboards creaked, his very bones creaked. But it was their bed that creaked the most, especially at night.

When every other sound was stilled, the creaks from their bed were easily audible through the wooden partition. When the creaking picked up a rhythm, a relaxed tempo at first, then quickening, building up a crescendo, he tried hard not to imagine them making love. But his greatest difficulty on such nights was reaching the toilet.

He found one slipper, but for the other he had to get down painfully on his arthritic knees to reach under the cot. How long could he withstand the pressure before he had to cross the room? Fifteen minutes, twenty at most? He prayed her nap would end before that.

On those nights, he waited as long as he could, long after the last creak signalling the climax had died, before starting on his trip. He sensed her awake, her resentful glare boring into his back, as he sidled against the wall in the darkness. And again, on the return trip, after he had relieved himself of the burden of his bladder.

'Why does he have to go two-three times in the night? Wants to have a look, I am sure. The dirty old man!' he once heard her tell his son, who thankfully ignored her, pretending to be asleep.

Should he sit or stand? The pressure was less if he stood, but if he walked, the creaking floorboards might awaken her. He decided to continue sitting.

Her bed creaked. Was she waking up? Or just turning over in her sleep?

Ultimately, it was blood that counted. Were it not for his son, he would be out on the narrow lanes of Kalbadevi, hungry and homeless. What choice at his age would he have competing for survival with street-smart urchins or desperate beggars or even starving mongrels? His son's heart would have quailed at the idea of abandoning him, and in one of the rare instances where he overruled his wife, had built this partition in the room to accommodate him. In a house with a single room, a closet of a kitchen and a closet of a bathroom, it was no mean sacrifice. He was indebted to his son for letting him have exclusive use of hundred square feet in a locality where a six hundred square feet living space was a luxury. Abhorring every moment of his presence, his daughter-in-law extracted revenge through a thousand little cuts. But he could bear everything—what needs did a seventy-five-year-old have? His side of the partition was his asylum, shielding him from her eyes full of spite, if not from her tongue.

No, he couldn't complain too much. He had a roof over his head, and food, meagre but regular, which meant he was better off than a hundred thousand other denizens of the city. He hadn't been able to hand down much to his son, apart from his wisdom of experience, and his frustration, both worthless. The poor fellow hadn't done well either; he did all he could to keep them afloat, delivering packages for a courier company to godforsaken parts of the city until late in the night. Had they been a little better off, perhaps even his daughter-in-law wouldn't hate him as much as she did. He could understand the frustration of thwarted dreams.

The bed creaked. And again. And again. The old man sat numb in shock as the creaking picked up a familiar tempo.

It couldn't be his son at this hour. Who then? A neighbour?

Her lover must have slipped in while he was napping. But surely she knew he could hear them. She was counting on his silence, on his tacit connivance. He held his head in his hands. It would be so easy for her to poison his son's ears against him if she put her mind to it: a word here, a word there, and he could lose whatever he had. And what would his son gain if he knew?

A spasm of pain shot through his groin. He couldn't delay it any longer. He rose tottering to his feet. The creaking grew vehement.

The problems of youth—fidelity, trust, jealousy, passion. His son would learn to deal with them on his own.

He threw aside the partition door and lurched through. 'Oh god.'

'Who the hell? You said no one...'

The old man staggered towards the toilet fumbling with the drawstring of his pyjamas. The problems of old age were different.

When he was old, his son would come to realize that sometimes the biggest problem in life could be reaching the bathroom on time.

•◆

Love

Morning Showers

BISHWANATH GHOSH

'You know something,' she said, 'whenever it rains all of a sudden, something good happens to me.'

'Really?'

'When the postman came with the appointment letter for this job, it had just rained that afternoon.'

'And you started believing in it?'

'No, wait. Not just that. Many years ago, dad was in hospital. He had a heart attack. We were in Chhattisgarh then. There was only one small hospital there, a government hospital. Doctors said the only way to save him was to fly him to Delhi. How we managed to get into the plane is another long story, but the moment we landed in Delhi, it began to rain. And you know what? The doctors in Delhi refused to believe that he had had a heart attack. He was perfectly fine.'

'And you started believing in it?'

'Don't make fun of it,' she playfully punched his arm.

So that night when it suddenly began to rain soon after they had ended up doing what they shouldn't have, considering that she was another man's wife, he was surprised as well as relieved.

'Do you hear that? It's raining,' he whispered to her. She didn't respond. She lay clinging to him, absent-mindedly drawing invisible geometrical figures on his bare chest.

'Do you hear that? It's raining,' he said again. This time she looked up at him shyly, her face glowing in the darkened room. She smiled at him and nodded. They locked their lips and bodies once again and rolled over, trampling upon the guilt-bug that was lurking on the bed.

When he woke up, he found her arm around him. She was wide awake. Their cheeks were touching and her big, beautiful eyes were fixed at him. The gaze, at any other time of the day, would have made him feel smug. But right now it unnerved him.

'You are up already?' he asked.

'I didn't sleep at all.'

'Why?'

'Because I was busy looking at you. You looked cute.'

'Come on,' he blushed. 'What's the time now?'

'Wait,' she said and reached for her mobile phone that was lying behind her. In the process, she let him have a good look at her breasts, something that she had refused outright the night before. She had made it clear that she would remove her clothes only if the lights were off, or else he could forget about the whole thing. So they had spent the entire evening in near darkness, guided by the dim light coming from the next room. But now, bare under the streaming sunlight, she made no attempt to cover herself.

'Seven-twenty,' she said. As she checked the time, he couldn't help notice that the phone showed fourteen missed calls. She pressed the key to find out who all might have called her, and they all turned to be from one number, identified as 'Hubby'. From the corner of her eye she noticed he was watching, and she quickly pressed the 'exit' button and flung the phone away.

'Why didn't you answer his calls?' he asked.

'Because I didn't want to. That's why I kept the phone on silent mode.'

'But won't he be worried? You've been missing for the night.'

'I want him to be worried. I have lost count of the nights I worried about him.'

'So you want to get even with him.'

'Yes, can't I?'

'Using me as the tool?'

'Shut up, I love you. If I had to sleep with someone just to get even, I would've done that long ago. Do you think there would be any dearth of men for me?'

'I didn't mean that way.'

She now pulled up the sheet and covered herself. He got up and walked, naked, to the door to collect the morning's newspapers.

The only other flat on that floor was mostly locked, so there was no problem opening the door a little while being naked and stretching out the hand to pull in the newspapers. He subscribed to two newspapers, *The Hindu* and *The Economic Times*. He glanced at the front page of *The Hindu* as he shut the door. A cyclone was headed in the direction of Chennai. Heavy rains were predicted.

He slapped the newspapers next to her. She lay there motionless, her gaze fixed at the ceiling. He didn't feel like indulging her. He put on his clothes and went to the kitchen to make tea. In the fridge, he found three eggs. While the water boiled, he chopped an onion and two green chillies to make an omelette. While the tea leaves infused and the egg-white broke into small bubbles on the pan, he toasted four pieces of brown bread. He carried the breakfast tray and placed it on top of the newspapers. She was still looking at the ceiling.

'Look,' he said, 'I have never done this even for my wife. Do you mind getting up and eating something?'

'Why, do you think you are doing me a big favour?'

'Not a favour. I am just being nice. Now please get up.'

She sat up, holding the sheet tightly around her throat so that it didn't come off.

'What's this fuss about? I have seen you naked. Now what's the big deal?'

'Oh, shut up! You have not seen me naked.'

'Of course, I have.'

'No, you haven't.'

'But I have.'

'Okay, whatever. Where's the ketchup?'

When he got back from the kitchen, she was not there on the bed. He heard water running in the bathroom. He lit a cigarette and drank his tea. But hers was getting cold, and that was now irritating him. He rarely made tea, even for himself, and now that he had presented an entire breakfast on the tray, she had chosen to go to the bathroom. Couldn't she have gone to the bathroom before, or a little later? When the bathroom door opened, she emerged fully clad, just like she was the evening before, and sat in a corner of the bed in a dignified manner.

'Could you pass me my plate, please?' she said. She smelt of his soap.

'But the tea has gone cold.'

'Oh is it? Don't bother, I can't drink it hot anyway.'

'Are you sure?'

'I told you, don't bother.'

'Are you mad about something, something I said?'

'Why should I be mad? What for? All men are the same.'

'All men? But what did I do?'

'You did nothing. When did I ever say you did anything?'

'But you sound angry.'

'Not at all,' she said, as she daintily took a bite of the bread and omelette. 'Why should I be angry? You men are the same.'

Since she was fully clothed now, he suddenly felt like disrobing her and making love to her once again. But he didn't have the courage. She was sitting on the edge of the bed, in a ladylike fashion, eating her breakfast. He tried arousing her by placing his foot on her right shoulder and ticking her ear with his toes.

'Hello! What do you think you are doing?' she snapped at him, shaking his leg off. 'Can't you see I'm eating?'

He felt a bit embarrassed and withdrew his leg. 'I am sorry. It is just that I was overcome by affection.'

'Affection, my foot! All you men want is sex.'

'Why do you keep saying "You men"? I don't know about the other men in your life, but I certainly was not keen on the sex part.'

'Oh yeah? And you want me to believe that?'

'I swear on God.'

'You don't have to say anything. I know what you mean. I know you men.'

'You are getting me all wrong,' he said.

'I'm getting you right.'

'But what did I do? Did I do or say something to piss you off?'

'Nothing. It's just that I love my husband.'

'Then why didn't you take his calls? He kept calling all night.'

'That's none of your business.'

He saw her off at the elevator and said, 'Bye, Meenakshi.'

She did not reply, nor did she look at him. She pretended to be fiddling with her bag as the elevator doors shut. Only last evening, she had told him, 'Stop calling me Meenakshi. I am Meenu for you.'

He stood at the window and watched her drive out in the rain.

He stood there till the tail-lights, looking redder than ever, had become indistinguishable dots. He lit up another cigarette and picked up *The Hindu*.

•◆

Heartbreakers

PARITOSH UTTAM

Abhay had never been a hiking and trekking person. So he had a foreboding that something would go wrong on this trip that Rakesh was trying to persuade him to come to.

'But you know I never go on these camping trips, man,' Abhay said.

'Come on, just this once,' Rakesh said. 'We are all meeting after a year's gap after our graduation. Do you know how difficult it was to coordinate and get everyone to agree upon a date and place?'

'I know, but why not meet at a simple dinner or a get-together at a restaurant or at someone's house? Why go tramping in the hills in this monsoon and run into snakes and leopards and...'

'...And gorillas and anacondas too! We will be twenty kilometres from the outskirts of Pune, not deep in the heart of the Amazon rainforest. We will be lucky to see even a few monkeys. Don't be a sissy now. It's an easy track; even the girls can do it easily. The whole gang will be there. Manoj, Asif, Mona, Aruna, Priyanka...'

'Aruna? When did she become part of the gang?'

Abhay knew he was fighting a lost battle. There was too much peer pressure to withstand, especially when he did not have any excuse to wriggle out. He was free during the weekend; not only his parents but also his grandparents were hale and hearty, and not one watch-able movie was running in the halls. And Rakesh was aware of all these facts.

The trip started off well. The day was bright and clear; no threatening clouds loomed on the horizon despite the weather forecast; and for once, everyone turned up on time. Also for once, Rakesh had been truthful: the trail had a gentle slope, and they hardly encountered any wildlife but for a bunch of chattering monkeys. Towards the evening, Abhay as much as admitted to Rakesh that he was glad that Rakesh had convinced him to come.

Rakesh, who was the organizer-in-chief of the trip and the most enthusiastic trekker of the group, called for a halt. 'Guys,' he said, 'this clearing is a good spot to put up our camp for tonight. It will be dark soon. So let's gather some firewood from around here for our campfire.'

Abhay groaned inwardly. This campfire was just for the sake of having one. Rakesh could not imagine a trip without one. Meanwhile, Rakesh was busy dividing the group into pairs and sending them off into different directions to gather firewood.

'Manoj and Priyanka, that side; Asif and Mona, over there… just remember, only the dry wood. Don't break off green branches from the trees for god's sake. All sizes, big or small. Abhay and Aruna, that side, and I will go there. Be back here in thirty to forty five minutes, max. All clear?'

Abhay moved off in the indicated direction, then remembered to look around for his partner and was startled by her expression. She was staring at him and had turned pale.

'Are you okay?' Abhay asked. 'Shall we go?' She nodded, wordlessly, and followed him.

When they returned forty minutes later, with a bare handful of twigs, Rakesh blew his top. 'Where the hell were you guys? Got lost or what? And that's it, those five sticks between the both of you?'

Abhay went up to him and whispered fiercely in his ear. 'I will kill you tomorrow, I swear.'

The next day, when Abhay confronted Rakesh at his home, Rakesh drew back in fear. 'What did I do? I thought you had a good time.'

'I did. Until you sent Aruna with me…' 'So what?'

'So what? When I found myself alone with her, I was shocked to see her face—she had turned red, she was blushing, her lips were quivering, and eyes unable to look up straight. My first thought was that she was going to faint, and then, I realised with horror, that she was expecting me to propose to her. Everybody likes Aruna, but no one loves her. She's good, she's nice, but I'm afraid, that's all. She's one girl from whom the guys wouldn't run away if she came with a rakhi. I never had an inkling she felt that way about me. It was breaking my heart to see her standing there and praying that I would propose because she would never have the courage. So I proposed somehow, stammering and stumbling, because of course I didn't want to.'

'You what?'

'You heard me. God knows what she would do if I didn't. I simply couldn't break her heart.'

'And then what?'

'Then what? She accepted of course, you fool.'

Rakesh was incapable of asking anything further because he had collapsed to the ground, convulsed with laughter.

'Mona!'

'Aruna!'

The girls embraced and wept over each other's shoulders for

a few minutes. After recovering from their emotional discharge, Mona began, 'You naughty girl! No one ever had the faintest clue you felt that way about Abhay.'

Aruna smiled. 'Mona, can you keep a secret? Actually, I never felt that way about him.'

Seeing Mona's shocked face, she hurried on, 'I saw Abhay whispering to Rakesh. Immediately after that, Rakesh sent just the two of us to one side. I understood then that Abhay had arranged this because he wanted to propose to me. I was shocked, I think I turned as red as a beetroot. Sure enough, the poor fellow was staring at me, not knowing how to begin. And soon, he was proposing, stammering and stuttering. I felt so sorry for him, I mean, usually he's so smart and confident, you know. Good God, I never knew he loved me so much.'

'And so you accepted?'

'I had to. How could I say no? It would have broken his heart.'

'Oh Aruna!'

'Mona!'

The girls hugged again.

◆

Love... In a Fast Lane

AHMED FAIYAZ

The older generation feels that women of my generation are frivolous in relationships. They believe that we youngsters fall in and fall out of love very quickly. What can we do? We have so many options, and with time it doesn't get easier. Our lives are definitely more complicated! The latest *Cosmobabe* survey says that sixty per cent girls, in the age group of eighteen to twenty-four, in urban India have been in more than three relationships. That's going to freak out the uncles and aunties, isn't it? But it's good for us. Finally, we can pick and choose, unlike most women in the generations before us. Anyway, let me tell you a bit about my life since you seem quite interested. We'll get to the relationships bit quickly as I imagine that's what you want to hear about.

I grew up in Bangalore and finished college at St. Theresa's. Let's skip college life as my memory is a bit blurry. I'm a bit mixed up on who I went out with and when. It doesn't matter now really, does it?

Let's get to my first serious relationship. After college, I joined Adam, Smith and Jones, the advertising agency, as a client servicing executive. I began at the bottom of the ladder and worked very hard at it. I also quite enjoyed working there and doing what I did. Working with the creative team and the clients was very interesting. The client I handled was a French luxury brand, Paul & White that had launched a range of fragrances and apparel in the Indian market. At work, I grew close to my boss, Nishant Prasad who was the Manager handling this client, and a couple of others. There was nothing exceptional about him. I didn't feel an instant attraction towards him, but he was my first boss and he took me under his wing and showed me the ropes. I guess that sort of built familiarity. He was hardworking and grounded, unlike some pretty boys I went out with, in school and college. We worked long hours together, often ate lunch together and went out for coffee every other day. Before I knew it we were in a relationship. It was convenient and easy, given that we shared the same space at work. It went down well at the Agency, they seemed to encourage and support an office romance between co-workers. I guess it helped staff retention in some way.

After being together for over a year, we began having trouble. Nishant had come home and had met my parents, while I had no clue about his family and where he lived. He'd become edgy when we spoke about it and brushed away the topic saying that his parents were orthodox and they wouldn't understand. Through a friend at work I got to know that he was meeting girls in his community to get married and settle down. It was something he never admitted to even when I confronted him.

'Why do you believe these rumourmongers? My parents are forcing me to see girls. I'm just meeting them and rejecting all of them, one by one. Give it time and let me work things out,' he promised.

'Why can't you just tell your parents? Look, I'm not saying let's get married. I'm only twenty-three! I have a couple of years before I can think about settling down. But what's the harm in letting them know that you are in a committed relationship.'

'It isn't easy for me to just tell my parents! My Appa is very traditional in his beliefs; no one in my family has had a love marriage.'

'Why didn't you think of that when you began dating me Nishant? Didn't your Appa and his rules play in your head back then? Why can't you just stand up for yourself?' I said feeling annoyed at his lack of courage.

'Relax Manpreet, I'm asking you to give me some time yaar! Look baba, the office trip to Coorg will give us some much-needed time together,' he added in a conciliatory tone.

'I'm not going!' I said storming out of his cabin.

I didn't go that weekend and this thawed our relationship a bit.

We kept it cordial and kept up appearances. We still had lunch and hung out in office together. We went out for the occasional movie and coffee. He continued to drop me home from work. I also heard from a college friend that Nishant's family had proposed to a cousin of hers! My friend, who knew about his relationship with me, asked her cousin to turn him down. I was shaken but I didn't confront him.

The problem was that he was still my boss, and anything I said or did, could also complicate our work situation. I didn't want to leave my job or quit the team; I enjoyed what I did. Nishant also began to travel a lot to Delhi as he was managing a telecom client for the Agency who had just begun offering their services in Delhi.

He had left Paul & White for me to manage since I'd been working with them for a year and was in sync with their team and their expectations.

At a meeting to discuss the campaign for a new fragrance called Gray by Paul & White, I met Raghav Nanda. He was a Manager at

Media Q, our sister Agency who handled Media Planning.

Our agencies often worked on the same clients and pitched for work together. Raghav was very self-assured and articulate. I was impressed by how he managed the client and convinced them to go with the plan he had put together. After the presentation at Paul & White's office in Indiranagar, he came up to me.

'I haven't seen you before. I've always dealt with Nishant on the Paul & White account. Thanks for chipping in and supporting my arguments,' he said with a charming smile.

'No worries, you were really good,' I said returning the smile and picking up my folder to leave.

'How did you get here? We could get back to office together. Maybe grab lunch before that?'

'Sure, sounds good. I'm quite hungry,' I said taking off my blazer.

Raghav had a lean frame and was over six feet tall; he had curly hair and seemed like a very easy going guy. 'I haven't seen you around at the Agency. I've been here for a year,' I said.

'I just moved here from Mumbai last month. I worked there for a couple of years after my MBA. It's good to get away from the madness. You could point me in the right direction here,' he added with a beguiling smile, 'Are there any nice places to eat in this neighbourhood apart from the usual burger-pizza joints?'

'Casa Picola nearby is quite nice. I used to go there a lot during college,' I said remembering the good times.

'So you're a Bangalore girl huh?' he asked warmly as we got into the elevator.

'Yes, I am. I've been here all my life! It's a lot more crowded now than it used to be.'

'Yeah, a lot of people say that. I came here last when I was a kid and it was a completely different place. It seems like there was more peace and tranquillity back then.'

'It still has its tranquil spots. But what brings you here? Do you have any family in Bangalore?' I asked with interest while we got into his shiny new Swift.

'No, my parents live in Mumbai, and so does my fiancée...' he said turning his gaze away from mine.

'It's difficult for you then. Why did you move?'

'I actually asked to be moved. It's quite complicated; well everyone's life is today...I just wanted to get away and get some space,' he said candidly.

'Can life ever be simple?'

'You've just stepped out into the real world! What could possibly be the complication in your life?' he asked turning to look at me, feigning a look of surprise.

I hesitated for a moment and said, 'I'm in a relationship with Nishant who doesn't quite have the guts to talk to his parents about us. He's busy seeing women for marriage...'

'You're young and beautiful...get out of it before it destroys you. There's so much more you could look forward to,' he said in a contemplative tone.

'It isn't that simple; we like each other and we also work together. He's my boss. I don't want to quit my job you know.'

'You're in a comfort zone. Don't worry so much, you've only just begun working. You'll find something else; there are many good agencies in town. You seem like you enjoy what you do.'

'You've given me something to think about,' I said, looking out of the window, 'Turn right here and park ahead.'

We walked over to Casa's and enjoyed a quiet meal. We spoke about the Agency and our respective jobs, and bitched about some of the higher-ups in the Agency. He was suave and intelligent; he had a way with words. He soon began to flirt with me, which I found odd considering what he had told me moments ago.

'Tell me about your complications. Why are you in Bangalore?' I asked while browsing through the menu.

He looked at me for a moment and said, 'Well I don't know, Sanjana and I have been seeing each other for a couple of years. We've been engaged for a year and I'm not sure if marrying her is the best thing for me.' His phone beeped and he quickly replied to a message which I presumed was from her.

'How did she take you moving here?' I asked.

'She did moan about it, and asked me to consider other options. But this is my way of buying time till I figure out what is best for me. I know she doesn't want to leave her spoilt life in Maximum City and move here,' he said with a wry grin.

'You men na! Honestly, why keep her dangling? She seems to be committed to you.'

'I'm sure she is; I'm not sure if I am. In the recent past we've had a lot of differences. We don't seem to be sorting anything out. For her life is all about the latest designer bag, tasting wine, shopping everyday and travelling to exotic locations. She's quite high maintenance and I don't know if I'm the guy for her. All she does is sleep, shop and have a good time. She keeps tabs on me all day on Facebook. This and constantly texting me to check where I am, and what am I up to.'

'You poor boy, you've ended up with quite a difficult sort.' From what he said she seemed to be a bored, spoilt and obsessive sort.

'Anyway, what are you up to tonight? Let's go somewhere; show me some nightlife in your sleepy city.'

'Sure, where do you stay? I'm not doing anything much tonight.'

I didn't care what Nishant thought, he was away in Delhi anyway.

'I have an apartment in Langford Town. Is that far away from where you stay?'

'It's quite close by actually; I'm at Richmond Town with my family. You could pick me up tonight and we could go to Blue Bar.'

'Sounds like a plan,' he said while picking up the check.

We went out to Blue Bar that night. I got quite wasted and we had a nice time on the dance floor. He wasn't stuck up like Nishant and went with the flow, moving really well and matching his steps with mine. The conversation was easy and we got quite intimate with each other. We ended up making out in his car after we left the lounge. He dropped me back home, and we met for brunch the next morning at Koshy's.

'I feel we are moving a bit too quickly, don't you think?' I asked.

'Why do we have to think through and plan everything?' he retorted. He looked relaxed and unperturbed in his cargo shorts and a casual shirt.

'Well let's see, you're engaged, and I'm seeing Nishant, at least for the moment…'

'We are both unhappy with our partners. Let's just go with the flow and take it as it comes….'

'But what does that make us? Where do we stand, you and I?' I asked trying to come to terms with our situation.

'We're two people who are attracted to each other, and who enjoy spending time with each other. Cheers to us!' he said clanking his cup of coffee with mine.

I managed to smile, though I was a bit confused. I knew I was getting into something complicated. Raghav certainly didn't act like he would end up marrying Sanjana, and the night before was the best night I had had in a long time.

After brunch we drove over to his place and spent a lazy afternoon in his apartment. He told me everything about Sanjana; how they met at a common friend's party and began seeing each other. It was almost like he was thinking aloud and putting to words his doubts for the first time. He had started to notice how obsessive she was over the past one year and had begun to have second thoughts. He said he needed this time away to really figure things out.

I couldn't completely trust either of them. Nishant seemed to care about me and seemed like the safe bet while I was quickly falling in love with Raghav despite everything else.

Murmurs about Raghav, whom I began to affectionately call Randy, and me were the latest gossip. I'm sure we were the headliners in many a hurried session by the water cooler and during smoke breaks. I was having a great a time and so was Randy. It was something he was accustomed to, and he enjoyed the attention. He liked being known as the office stud. I enjoyed the spotlight too, it was something else being wooed and being in a relationship with two of the most eligible men in office. It seems like I was quite a slut when I think about it now. I would have lunch with one guy and then coffee with another. I would then go for dinner with one of them and see the other one at a lounge on Friday or Saturday night.

One day, Nishant confronted me over lunch in his cabin. It was the usual takeaway fried rice and a chicken in hot garlic sauce from Beijing Bites down the street.

'What's all this chatter about you and that Raghav Nanda? I don't like what I'm hearing and I have a feeling people are laughing at me behind my back. Is there something you want to tell me?' he asked raising his voice.

'Randy is a good friend and we're working on the Paul & White launch campaign together. You can't tell me what to do and who to hang out with!' I found it funny that many of his colleagues were snickering about him. He went from being known as the rising star, the cool dude who went out with the pretty girl at work, to being called the office loser.

'I have a right to ask! People think I'm a joke! You and I are in a relationship at the end of the day,' he said worriedly.

'I can't control what people think at work. Besides, you should have thought about your relationship with me before going and proposing to Smita's cousin. It's strange how you remember that you are in a relationship just when you see me spending time with another guy!'

'I did not...' I got up and walked out of his cabin before he could complete his sentence. I went down to the fourth floor where Randy's office was. He was on the phone and hung up when he saw me walk in. I drew the blinds in his cabin and flung myself into his arms and drew his lips into mine. It was only him in my life from that moment.

The same weekend, Randy and I walked in together for the office Christmas party. We stayed together through the evening, and got on the dance floor where we passionately kissed for a while as we got up close on the dance floor. I could see Nishant turning a deep red and leaving the party when he saw us in a clinch. It was exactly the way I wanted it. He was doomed to be the office loser for the rest of his life. He had been humiliated and dumped unceremoniously in full public view.

On Monday, following the weekend I was called into Nishant's cabin. 'It seems like you had a wonderful weekend,' he said seething with anger, when I walked in.

'I can see you did too,' I said with a smile which seemed to irk him even more.

'You damn slut! You could have ended things with me if you wanted to. Why did you have to make a public spectacle of our relationship?' he said in a voice filled with pent-up rage.

'Screw you! You better watch the way you speak to me. You

don't want to be hearing from the Head Office in London for misbehaving with me, do you?' I said in an intimidating voice.

He took off his glasses and ran his hand through his rapidly receding hairline. 'I'm transferring you to Vasant's team. He will be handling Paul & White from today, please go and give him a briefing about the client and the work you've been doing,' he said calming down and sipping a glass of water.

I saw very little of him after that. He moved to Delhi after a month and I hear he got married to someone his Appa picked out for him. He seems to have got what he wanted and deserved in life.

Time to go people... Raghav is here already. We are heading out to watch the latest Twilight movie. And oh, last week he dumped that high maintenance fiancée of his. That's how easy it is with us, we fall in love easily, we move on quickly. Now I'm wondering what to wear...

•◆

Serendipity

PARITOSH UTTAM

Leather-back *Crime and Punishment* slips from drowsy fingers, strikes the floor plangently, nudging the sleeper from intermittent slumber into wakefulness. He looks vaguely upwards at the wall and as if in anticipation, the clock answers in twelve metronomic chimes. Surmounting inertia after a brief struggle, he sits up on the four-poster and surveys his surroundings.

Shoes, socks, shirt and underwear embellish the carpet, the last three turned inside out. Dark olive green Budweiser has found its niche amidst the legs of the dining table and the chairs. The uncluttered portion of the table exposes its grimy face shamelessly to the sunbeams the curtains have failed to keep out. Grim resolutions of reprimanding and dismissing the maid-servant gestate within Abhishek.

Self-exhortation succeeds in pushing him into the bathroom where he stands before the mirror coaxing toothpaste out of the tube and finds that his face is in no better condition than the room he has just scrutinised. Dark half-rings support his eyes from below, overgrown moss-like stubble smothers his cheeks and jowl; his hair stand in uprising against the comb, daring it to lay them down again.

Abhishek flinches from the apparition in the mirror, but then boldly accosts him. 'You spineless invertebrate,' he begins tautologically, 'is this what you so presumptuously call your life? You are twenty-seven, single, have a bank balance of six figures (seven, counting your stock options) and can make yourself look presentable unless you are against deforestation. Surely, even you realise that there is something missing in you?'

But the apparition is no pushover; it is ready with its laterally inverted answers. 'That bank balance,' it responds, 'which you throw so disdainfully at my incorporeal face, has come about because I battle deadly traffic from Marathalli to MG Road every morning, and also stay back late nights working to meet impossible deadlines to please my boss. How then, pray tell me, do I find the time to look after myself? Only during weekends can I indulge in pleasures like reading, drinking and watching TV.'

It ignores Abhi's cynical chuckles and murmurs of 'excuses' and continues, 'Yes, I know what is missing. A girl, woman, female, distaff—that is what is lacking, a feminine presence. There are colleagues in the office, but I don't want to talk Java Beans and Active Server Pages and Object-Oriented Programming concepts, I want to talk about...' he indicates the tome spreadeagled on the carpet, 'about Dostoyevsky. I want to wake up in the morning, turn to her supine form beside me, shake her shoulder gently and ask, 'Why do you think Raskolnikov killed the moneylender?'

'The question why Raskolnikov killed the moneylender,' she tells the class, 'is to be seen as a specific instance of a larger question—can one kill another for the sake of a principle? But the fundamental question that Dostoyevsky poses here is whether evil means ultimately justify noble ends. What do you think, Ganesh?'

Ganesh has been keeping himself updated with the progress of the India-Australia match with his GPRS-enabled Samsung Corby and would rather have answered a query on Sachin Tendulkar's cricketing statistics. Gently tossing her braid over her shoulder, she glides on however, without expecting an answer. She knows she is not the teacher who galvanizes her students into action, or one who inspires respect, but one who barely passes muster.

She passes muster because she ignores proxy attendance, never flunks students, who in turn do not bother her in the class. It is a give and take of mutual indifference for she knows they are not vying for a B.A. degree in BES College, Jayanagar, out of choice; that most days they spend in computer training classes in the hope of landing a job in one of the thousands of IT companies teeming in the city. Thus, she paces countless steps up and down the aisle until the class ends, in her grey sari that makes her look as uninteresting as the flat tone in which she reads out a passage from *Crime and Punishment*, which she has chosen as part of the 'Reading the Novel' syllabus.

Predilection for Dostoyevsky and Russian literature wins her the epithet Comrade Protimov in the staff room. It is there she takes her unvarying two chappatis-rice-dal-curd-pickle lunch prepared by maternal hands, because her culinary skills, like the didactical, only pass muster. She prefers not to walk twenty minutes in sun or rain to her house where her mother will pound her continually with well-intentioned homilies on the merits of connubial life.

Piscine odour assails her olfactory senses causing her to wrinkle her nose in disgust, the reaction noticed by her staff room neighbour Mary Verghese, whose lunch box is the source of the offending smell. 'Why don't you take non-veg?' she goads Protima.

'Because I think it is a sin to kill animals for one's food,' the vehemence in her reply surprises both speaker and listener. But Madam Verghese rallies strongly, with what she is convinced is an irrefragable argument. 'But don't you kill plants for your food? Are they not living?'

Gamely, Protima attempts to carry on what she knows will end a futile exercise. 'The issue here is of conscious and avoidable cruelty, not...' but her opponent's sneer halts her in mid-sentence.

'...not quibbling about what is living and what is non-living,' he finishes, pushing his plate away, which fortunately he has emptied, and so doesn't lose his lunch along with his temper. 'Fish is nothing but the vegetable of the sea, indeed!'

Nisupta Biswas withers under his fiery gaze. And this is the girl, his colleague, on whom he had decided to bestow affectionate looks, instead of indifferent glances because... because their cubicles are adjacent, they are thrown in together for hours at work, and have lunch at the same table in the cafeteria.

Abhishek is conscious that he has been trying to force a jigsaw piece fit into a pattern to which it does not belong; Nisupta Biswas has nothing in common with him but for their reporting manager. Also, there is an underlying awareness that while earlier he used to mentally classify women as attractive or plain, for some time now he has been involuntarily assessing how well they would blend in his hypothetical homestead.

Such assessments are not limited to the precincts of the office, but are processes that are carried out subconsciously on faces glimpsed while walking in the streets, on salesgirls in shopping malls, even on fashion models on TV or billboard advertisements. Strangers are sized up, their looks evaluated, characters appraised, tastes conjectured at, and a final rating on a scale of ten calculated, much in the manner his performance in the office is rated.

Scattered somewhere in the memory of his computer resides a document named *My_Ideal.doc* that contains a lexicographically ordered set of phrases, which he compiles whenever he finds both leisure and inspiration. Like a police artist drawing a picture from the witness' description, he strives for a picture in his head: but his agnostic, crossword-solving, Dostoyevsky-Kafka-Sartre relishing, height five feet four inches and weight fifty-two kilogram, knowing-just-enough-cooking-not-to-set-the-kitchen-on-fire, narrow-waisted, one year younger, quiz-freaking, short-haired, vegetarian-only dieting woman easily evades his tenuous net of imagery. Sometimes he thinks he has succeeded in capturing her, but it is a mere silhouette; the details, the colours, elude him.

In Robert Bruce fashion, he begins all over again, starting with her hair. His penchant for the bob cut gives her a boyish flat sweep of hair in front, cropped close and tapering at the nape. Stepping back, he regards his mental handiwork with satisfaction.

The hairdresser in Liu's Beauty Parlour, Residency Road, is indeed satisfied with her hour-long diligence. 'You are done, Madam,' she informs Protima. 'The mushroom cut really suits you.' Protima regards the mirror as she would a stranger; her mother would need some convincing before she lets her into the house. But at least it would give her mother something else to think about other than tirelessly accumulating marriage proposals for her.

Perseverance is a trait of the Mathurs, and Protima admits that however nettlesome her mother might sound, she has got a point, or even two—that Protima is twenty-six and can only grow older, that her chances of getting married became inversely proportional to her age once she crossed twenty-four, that she can do her Ph.D even after marriage, that at this very moment, she has three proposals on the hold only awaiting the slightest affirmative sign from Protima.

Equally steadfast in refusing every one of them is Protima, who, to please her mother, peruses the biodatas received in response to the advertisement placed in *The Times of India* surreptitiously by the latter, but as she expects, finds nothing in them that she can relate to. What she expects is not fair, she confesses; the day she finds the man who can express his life in one and a half typewritten, double columned, foolscap sheets, she vows she will marry him.

Her mother, Protima is thankful, is technologically challenged, and hence cannot pursue online alternatives like *Shaadi.com* or *BharatMatrimony.com*.

Attractive men are not complete aliens to her; there are students almost her age whose looks she finds appealing, but who take to their heels if she as much as mentions existentialism; those who don't are the professors above fifty with grandchildren, and a third category she has not met on the campus. The attraction of opposites she dismisses as pure bunkum, a pretty figure of speech and nothing else. What really counts is the similarity of thoughts and tastes; similarity, she stresses, not identicalness. The only man she can relate to, she feels, is Dostoyevsky. She visualizes an exchange with her mother, 'Mamma, I like a man. He is a writer, a Russian, was a prisoner in a Siberian camp, and is dead for the last 130 years.' Her mother's reaction, she does not dare envisage.

Hoydenish hairdo causes consternation at home, staff room and classroom. But Mrs Mathur is surprisingly positive about the new look, hopeful that it is the harbinger of a new outlook in her daughter's that life can exist beyond the covers of her books. She even finds the way Protima sits and doodles over the crossword refreshing: with her back leaning against one arm-rest and legs dangling over the other; there is a bracing air of abandonment in her.

Protima, too, is sanguine—she has won a place in the semi-finals of the Mastermind Quiz and is to go to New Delhi by flight—she has never been on a plane before. 'On an impulse,' she answers truthfully whenever she is asked why she cut her hair for it was an impulse that made her rush to Liu's Parlour as soon as she received the flight tickets and say, 'Cut it off, shear off as much as you can, I have to feel light because I am going to fly.' But 27 Across stymies her progress and brings her down to earth: Shadow fencing cannot alter their course when they begin to blow (5,2,6). She suspects it is an anagram and thinks with pencil-end-gnawing concentration.

WINDS OF CHANGE, he fills the white squares with neat capitals after reshuffling 'shadow-fencing' and shakes his head ruefully. The winds of change in his life cannot stir the lightest leaf.

Tomorrow morning he catches yet another flight to New Delhi, to meet yet another client to discuss yet another project. He shuts off all lights and goes out to the balcony and sees the full moon. It's been months, he recalls, since he has last seen it. The one compensation of flying is that on board, and in the waiting areas, he has the chance to finish reading the final two chapters of *Crime and Punishment* for the fourth time. Also on board, knee-length airhostess skirts will trigger off a mental slideshow of similar visions—all images that remind him with a pang of the absence of the feminine element in his life. In rapid succession, there will flit by minis and midis, shapely and stockinged legs, sandals and high heels, midriff skimming tops, shirts softly accentuating the contours of breasts, glabrous stretches of skin of cheeks and legs and underarms, heady mixtures of perfumes and deodorants inhaled furtively standing close by in elevators, and the palpable softness of handshakes.

Whenever he sees young couples walking hand in hand on Brigade Road, or giggling and winking at each other across a Cafe Coffee Day table, he tells himself that he is above and beyond such juvenile pleasures. He has to try hard to convince his alter ego, the apparition in the mirror, because he is scared that the unpalatable truth might be that he is too old already at twenty-seven. Unchanging and ugly as the pockmarked moon he watches sadly, he fears he will remain as lonely and isolated through the centuries.

Stately and splendid it will remain forever, she feels, watching the moon dreamily from her terrace. Her arm draws backwards on its own seeking support, but then suddenly, stops short. It is not mother's warm touch she needs now; she is looking for a firmer, broader, taller frame against which she can rest her head: a male chest, for example. The tall and broad shouldered owner of that chest would not speak, just his stable presence would suffice— were words needed between them and their moon? She blushes in the darkness, thankful no one can see her blush nor read the thoughts that make her blush, but she has just realized that her hero is quintessential Mills & Boon.

'Forgive me, Fyodor,' she murmurs, 'but your characters are not hero material. They are anything but dependable. Wouldn't you like it if I could depend on him totally, he being so well-off... I could chuck this stupid teaching job, and devote all my time to you?' And then, perhaps, even the thought of flying on the morrow will not seem as outlandish as it does now.

It could become as mundane to her as it is to the young man who stands in front of her the next morning, at the check-in counter.

'Window seat, please,' he says in an utterly bored voice that sounds as if he wishes he were at any place other than this swanky BIAL terminal.

'Window seat, please,' echoes Protima when her turn comes.

Flight 6E132, seat 22A, boarding Rear: she follows the instructions on her boarding pass dutifully.

The sudden, lurching acceleration of the aircraft just before the take off, and the sight of the earth falling away thrills her. Mid-flight, she realizes she has to visit the toilet: the first time, she makes a mental note, as she brushes past withdrawn knees and waits in the aisle for the OCCUPIED sign on the door to turn VACANT, at an altitude of 30,000 feet.

A cute haircut, Abhishek notes from the corner of his eyes as she walks to the rear. The young man in 21A, she observes indignantly, is reading. Why then did he ask for a window seat if he does not want to look out the window?

At the exit gates of the Indira Gandhi airport at New Delhi, while Protima ponders over the means of transport to avail to reach her destination at Lodhi Road, the young man saunters past her and waves at a chauffeur holding a placard with the name ABHISHEK CHOUDHURI. At that moment, she glimpses, the book the man clutches to his side with his elbow, and gasps, recognizing a replica of the leather bound *Crime and Punishment* she possesses.

The gasp is audible to Abhishek, who turns back to find the girl with the cute hair cut staring at him. For a full second, their eyes meet, and are filled with recognition. Then the second passes, they snap out of the magic moment shaking their heads with apologetic smiles; Abhishek follows his chauffeur, Protima heads for the prepaid taxi stand.

That's the closest they ever come to in each other's thoughts— as the young man in 21A who was too busy reading to admire the cotton clouds floating past under his nose, and as the cute haircut in the aisle who gave him a disdainful glance. For whatever power that decides the course of their lives has a sick sense of humour.

And yet, it is not bad, for it never lets them know either that they once came within six inches—seated, from her knees to his back—of their perfect mate.

•◆

Slow Rain

ABHA IYENGAR

As Meera opened her eyes, her first thought was to text Rakesh. 'Hi, how are you? It's raining here.' Then she snuggled in, listening to the rain.

The sound of the water dropping from the fibreglass awning over her window, the cooling of the room as she lay in late because it was a Sunday, the slow lethargy of unwinding from a deep and restful sleep, all added up to make her feel romantic and wanting to connect with him. Sometimes he was the only dream she had because the reality was what she had to live through and experience.

The kids ran into the room, wanting their Sunday morning breakfast. They fell over her. Their long ringlets tickled her face and she breathed their sleep in, holding on to them tight and thankful, so thankful for their being there.

The bell rang and they ran off now, shouting, 'Papa's back,' scampering for the door. She adjusted her sari and threw a passing look in the mirror, taking in her sleepy eyes and dishevelled hair. She ran a hand over her hair in an attempt to straighten it as she ran to the door. Yogi did not like waiting at the door. Yogi did not like waiting for anything, actually. He had rushed her into marriage and now was rushing around all the time, as though every minute of his life had to be worth something. He was always imbued with an adrenaline rush, for him the cigarette had to be smoked mighty fast, the breakfast gobbled up, the bathroom used and left at breakneck speed. The elevator had to move at the press of a button, otherwise... She had often watched him completely disintegrate if things did not happen pronto. Caught as she was in his whirlwind existence, it was only when she was away from him that she felt she could breathe.

She opened the door and saw her husband, back from his overnight office trip, one hand clutching the umbrella and the other a bag of groceries, picked up on his way home.

He was on time as usual but she had slept in late, trying to enjoy a lazy Sunday without him having her jump out of bed for an early morning walk with him. She had not been able to say a 'no', for he was just so pushy, she could not gather enough strength to push back and say her bit.

He thrust the bag of groceries in her hands and moved in. The children saw him, said their quick hellos and followed her into the kitchen. He had gone into the bedroom to strip down and change into another pair of clothes. He came out, running the towel through his hair and sat on the table, reaching for the morning papers. She had the coffee ready, quick, quick, the dosas spluttering on the pan, and the kids got busy, pulling at her sari, 'Amma, amma, we want dosas...'

Her children seemed to have inherited her husband's desire of wants and their immediate gratification. How she wished she could flutter in the wind without a care like the muslin curtains strung across the window seemed to be doing. She called out to him, 'Yogi, please call the kids,' sweat gathering on her brow despite the cool air wafting in. She heard his fingers drumming the table with impatience. He yelled to the kids and they scampered out of the kitchen, their eyes showing their hunger. They clambered onto his lap and he pushed them down, trying not to be rough and told them to get themselves a chocolate each from the stuff he had bought.

Meera always got distracted like this. Now she had to watch the dosas and make sure that the children not spill anything precious out of the bag in their hurry to grab some chocolate.

The kids grabbed the paper packets and spilled everything in the process. A strawberry jam jar rolled under the dining table and one of the kids ran to pick it up, the other chased her and they forgot about the chocolates. She looked at the spilt contents with dismay. Yogi's hurry never included clearing up a mess that he had initiated the makings of, that was her domain. Yes, domains were clear and marked. He slogged out of the house, she had to do her bit in here.

Not so long ago, Meera had wanted to put her hair up and dance, feel the breeze enter her body and caress it with longing. Instead, she now felt nothing but this rush and panic to get things done, even on a Sunday. Yogi could have claimed this day as his day of rest. He had excuse enough, for he had driven back from a late office meet in the city suburbs. He could have put his feet up and relaxed, but she knew he would not do it. He would have twenty things to be done lined up in his head and she would have to do them with him, or for him.

She had tried protesting in the early days of marriage, when she had still some spunk in her, and he had told her in no uncertain terms that that was his nature. He had not been brought up in a languid household like she had.

She had learnt that it was useless to complain for he would

refer to her small-town background with a jeer, even though her parents had moved out of there a long time ago and her father was a lecturer in the local university. Of course, her Sundays at home before her marriage had been different. They had been spent dreaming, reading and talking. She had spent Sundays cooking a meal slowly with her mother, whose eyes were watchful yet gentle like a deer. That is what had made Meera into a rather unhurried and fabulous cook, yet now she could not indulge in enjoying the process of cooking. It was just 'finish it off, finish it', and move on to the next chore.

She saw Yogi sitting on the table, his fingers drumming, his eyes restless. They darted from corner to corner as though hunting for some prey, something to grab which had to be done and immediately accomplished. She placed the cooked dosas in front of him and hurried in to make some more for the kids. Both the girls were busy playing with the jam jar and she decided to let her mind ignore the fact that the jam jar could break. Break into glass smithereens which may hurt her kids but she had had enough of being careful.

She really wanted to fling the ladle on to the dosa pan and leave, go out and feel the patter of the raindrops on her face, hold her arms out and get drenched in the rain, get completely and totally unhurried wet. She wanted to feel the sting of the rain against her skin like a lover's thousand kisses. She imagined Rakesh taking her right there in the middle of the rain in the middle of the garden, out in the open. She wished Yogi would see her then, her slow yielding and opening up, not the rapidness with which she participated in their lovemaking, the incessant pushing towards the finishing line.

She did not know how it would be with Rakesh, whether it would happen at all, but if it did, it would be different. Definitely slower. A relationship that built and developed over time, each brick allowed to bask and form completely in the sun, and laid with exquisite care over the other.

Rakesh was the owner of the bookshop down the road. The Cozy Bookshop was not a very inventive name, she had thought to herself wryly, when she had first come upon it. The Cozy Bookshop has soon become the place where she went sometimes to slow her pace and find some sanity from the whirling world of morning coffees, tiffin boxes, homework and dishes to be done. And from the sooty webs that hung to be cleaned forever, from the dust that gathered in crevices which continuous dusting could not remove. At the bookshop she could think again.

She would sit there engrossed over some book which she would consider buying, her one indulgence and it was not begrudged by Yogi, though he could never understand her need to lose herself in words when the whole world was waiting to be related to and dealt with. He was always engrossed in the present moment, in the doing rather than the being. They lived in a world of non-comprehension, he of hers and she of his, yet they did try to make it work. Actually, she had to make it work and gear herself up to his demands and requirements. He had a choice whether he wanted to accept her wishes or not and often put his foot down on things he was not interested in her doing. So going to the bookshop had become, for her, the sanctioned haven.

Rakesh, with whom for a long time she just had a nodding acquaintance, had walked up to her one day as she sat on one of the low stools. She was considering which next fantasy novel to pick for the coming Saturday, a day when Yogi would be away.

Rakesh, walking up to her then, had asked, quite casually, whether she liked Bacigalupi.

'Never heard of him,' she said, instantly, her interest in writers and writing making her forget that she did not usually talk to other men. She looked up to him, and noticed the red tilak on his forehead, the fair skin, the beard, the hair slicked back from an early balding forehead and warm twinkling eyes. He had his hands in the pockets of his jeans, a faded army green and not the usual blue, and his t shirt stuck tight to his body. He was also quite a tall man, so she had to look up quite a length.

She wished suddenly that she was not so petite, something she had not really thought about till now. Another thought crossed her mind, 'He seems a devout Hindu. One of those ultra-religious types. And he reads fantasy?'

'Ah, a frown on that forehead,' he said. 'Something crossed your mind? Are you wondering about the author?'

'Yes,' she hedged, 'I would love to read something by him , if you have it.'

'It has just come in, his latest book actually, and I think it's worth a read. I like fantasy myself.'

She found herself sharing. 'Actually I like all kinds of stuff, but I think at present fantasy helps.'

'It does?' He looked at her and grinned. 'It always does help, anytime of your life.'

So they began the sharing of stories and writers and experiences and a friendship grew. She began to look forward to going to the bookstore even more than before, for reasons other than before. It became a place where she found herself slowing down, softening up, the quietness pervaded her being. Rakesh, when around, did not disturb her unless she looked up and smiled. Her smile would make him come over and then they would discuss reading and writing for a while.

For the last week, it had been raining. She had not gone browsing to the bookstore. And this morning she had woken up thinking of Rakesh. And she had sent him the text.

The kids broke into her thoughts. They were clamouring for a Sunday outing, the much promised boat ride and then pizzas and ice-cream at Nirula's. The rain had stopped, the sky had cleared, and Yogi was asking her to get ready. Yogi, despite all the driving he had done already, had no problems about braving the city traffic again.

She wanted to lie in bed and dream, read some newspapers, have a chocolate cookie and tea, but shook her head, yes, she would get ready. The kids began to jump up and down and she held their hands and took them into the bathroom with her, smiling. She bathed them and got them ready and told them to play outside while she quickly wore her sari, a new blue one.

The drive to the lake, on the outskirts of Delhi, was long. However, the weather was cool and balmy. At the lake, a couple of speedboats were available for hire. Yogi guided the boat skilfully through the waters and they watched the white spray fly behind them.

The mobile pinged. Meera took her gaze off the spray and her children. She looked at the message. It was from Rakesh. Her heart skipped a beat.

'Hi. Was thinking of u 2. Just married. Secret 4 d girl not Hindu. Sunny here in Tri. Talk 2 u soon. Tc.' Her head raced. Quite a lot had happened in a week of rain, she had not even known that Rakesh had gone away from the bookshop. To Trivandrum to get married! She was surprised that he had given no inkling of it, but then, they did not really share their private lives, only their bookish ones, she realized.

A slight drizzle had started. Yogi revved the speedboat back. She went up to him and said, 'Let me. Go sit with the girls.' There was an edge to her voice. He sensed the danger, something he had never encountered before, and, amazed, he stepped back. She turned the boat around, hard. Time to get back on track; she had slipped for a while in the promise of rain.

The rain came down in sheets.

'Fast enough, Yogi, to make it back in one piece?' she asked.

'You surprise me, Meera. Never thought...' his words were lost in the rain.

'It is a day of surprises.' Her voice was flat.

Through sheets of rain she sped it, this speedboat of her life. She wiped away the slow rain that fell on her cheeks.

◆

Friendship

Apple Pies and a Grey Sweater

PRATEEK GUPTA

Prayas walked into the apartment and turned on the lights. It had been a long and tiring day; one that he wished could be forgotten. To top a difficult day, he had to drive all the way from Hinjanwadi to Kothrud through the traffic snarl and the non-stop downpour, which took him over an hour to get home. An hour of crawling through the urban mess, where he had to work hard to keep his temper in check and avoid getting into an argument on the street. An aggressive motorist swerved dangerously across the street, causing him to brake suddenly, and resulted in an SUV bumping into him from behind. Fortunately it was just a fender bender, and nothing more.

Once home, he collapsed on the sofa, dialled the number of 'Fasoos', and ordered two kabab rolls. With dinner ordered, he decided to watch the news for a while. Life had become a tiresome routine. Drive to work, get through a day of monotony and get back feeling half-dead. He had no energy to do anything else. He remembered the good-old college days when he played basketball every other evening or went to the gym. He couldn't fathom how this could be possible now. He mulled over the idea of getting a bai to come and cook nutritious meals for him. His trousers had started to get tight, and his mother who had visited over the weekend, commented on how he had suddenly put on weight.

He saw the backlit display flashing on his phone. It was Purvi.

'Hi, how did you remember me at this hour? Isn't it time for *Friends* on TV?'

'I needed to talk to you about something,' she said in a pensive tone. She was the closest that he had to a girlfriend. Or possibly the closest he had come to having a girlfriend.

'Tell me. Is it raining in Bangalore as well? It's pouring cats and dogs out here,' he said, good-naturedly. He switched channels, the news on all the channels was about Akshay Kumar's birthday, and who all had called or given bytes to the media to wish him. Bloody rubbish, is this supposed to be news? He thought.

'I guess it was… in the afternoon. But Prayas, we need to talk about something.'

'Yes, I'm listening.'

'No you're not. You're watching the news, and commenting on it in your head. Turn it off for a few minutes.'

'Okay, done.' He stared at the blank screen and sat up, this seemed serious. They almost never had serious conversations. He wondered if she had gotten fired from her job at IBM. But she's doing pretty well, he thought.

'I'm getting married to Sanjay Rai. His parents are friends with my uncle and our horoscopes have also matched. He and I spent some time together on Sunday. The wedding is next month, and oh, he works at Oracle.' She almost hung up, after blurting out everything she had to say.

'What? You're getting married?' Prayas stood up with the mobile phone, and paced the room.

'Is that all you heard? Don't ask me to whom and where he

work. I told you that already.'

'No no, yes you did. Well, it's just a lot of information, suddenly. Congratulations!' he said nervously.

'Thanks.'

'Are you happy?'

'My parents are. It almost seems like they're getting married. Anyway, it's a relief, if anything. I've been made to see different guys every month. Sit there, smile, pretend, telling strangers where I went to college and what I like to cook. While my parents have been freaking out for a year, thinking that I'm growing old and I won't find anyone to settle down with.'

'Well, they must be elated.'

'Yes, the monkey's off their back. Sanjay is a nice guy, he's cultured, no-nonsense. My mother-in-law seems like a bitch, but I'm going to be in Bangalore, so that's good. It's a mixed bag.'

'Are you sure about it?'

'Are you coming for the wedding?'

'I don't know, send me the date, I'll try. I'll see if I can take off from work. These days…'

'Go to hell!' she said, cutting him short, and hanging up on him.

He decided not to call her back. He knew how she was when she got upset. He sat by the window sill and watched the rain wash the street outside his building. There was still a traffic jam outside, as cars honked at each other and crawled down the street, through bumper to bumper traffic. He remembered the first day he met her at their college fresher's party.

In Mumbai
4 years ago

Prayas was walking towards the dance floor in the lawn, when he heard a voice behind him. He had broken into a sweat and couldn't wait to go back and jive to the bhangra-pop.

'Run, take that drink for your madam quickly,' said the girl with the thick-rimmed glasses.

'Sorry.' Prayas stood there wondering what this was about. She was one of the better-looking girls in college. She spoke well and seemed sophisticated. He found her attractive, but she didn't look like she even noticed him in class. She didn't seem like she wanted any boy from college in her space. He saw her sitting opposite him with a grin on her face.

'That's for Namita right?' she said pointing at the drink in his hand.

'Yes it is.'

'Does she need two? I saw her ask Anil to also go and get her a drink.' Prayas looked downcast immediately.

'Come and sit here for a bit, she isn't missing you or the drink,' she said with a smile, turning to look at the dance floor. Prayas saw Namita gyrate with another guy from his class.

'Do you want a drink?' he asked, realising that he had two glasses of rum and coke in his hands.

'No I don't believe my boyfriend will appreciate the idea of me sitting here and drinking with you. I had a huge argument with him before coming to this party. It's the first time we've been apart na? He's a bit possessive. I didn't introduce myself, I'm Purvi.'

'I'm Prayas, basically from Jabalpur.'

'I'm from Bangalore. Now the reason I called you here is because I don't get it. Nice guys like you running behind Namita.'

'She's a nice girl…she's beautiful.' She gave him her piercing gaze, with a stern look on her face and then smiled.

'I guess the last part is true. She's my roommate; don't waste your time with her.'

'Why?'

'Why? Many reasons; or many guys I must say. Now you call her every other night, don't you? You went for coffee also, a couple of days back.'

'That's right.' Prayas looked pleased, one week into college and he'd already been on his first date.

'Yes, now there is her boyfriend, who is studying in Australia. Then, there's a local boyfriend, a former school friend who lives in Mumbai, with whom she sneaks out of the hostel and spends her nights with. Plus there is Anil, you and a couple of other guys who take her out for coffee. I mean given the number of guys what are the odds?'

'Are you serious? She told me she had never been out with a guy before she went with me for coffee.'

'Ha ha. Maybe she meant that she'd never been out with a guy from Jabalpur.'

'But she doesn't seem that way.' Prayas looked downcast. His dreams of dating the feisty Namita weren't looking good.

'Yes, she doesn't, and she won't seem that way to the guy she marries either. Her folks are conservative; they are planning to marry her off in the last semester itself.'

'Amazing, how could she lie to me?'

'And pop goes the balloon. Dude chill, she's having fun in life. You're the nice type, so I felt I'd let you know. You seem intense, and you shouldn't be falling for someone like her.'

'Can I get you anything at all?' He saw three guys trying to jostle for space next to Namita on the dance floor, as she got drunk by the minute.

'An orange or an apple juice please, if you don't mind.'

Prayas smiled as he chewed on his roll and took a sip of orange juice. She had saved him from wasting his time. He remembered the number of guys Namita dated in college and dumped, before getting married last month to some guy from her own community. He remembered getting an invitation from her, after which he called Purvi and laughed about it.

After that night at the Fresher's bash, they became fast friends. Prayas and she spent a lot of time together, going for movies and dinners, she found him to be simple and easy going, while he loved spending time with her.

A year ago
In Bangalore

Prayas turned on his mobile phone, as the aircraft taxied on the tarmac. Welcome to Bangalore, the temperature is a pleasant twenty-four degrees, the flight captain said on the radio.

'Hey, so what are your plans tonight?' he asked, smiling to himself.

'I just finished a family lunch. Why do you ask? It isn't like you're here…'

'Guess what? I am, and I will be for the next eight months. I've been seconded here on a long project.'

'What the…? Where are you going to be put up?'

'Some service apartment in Benson Town, I have it written down somewhere.'

'Okay, that's not too far from Koramangla.'

'Cool, I will go drop my bags off, change and meet you at Bangalore Central by 6:30 p.m.?'

'Ha ha, you fool! Do you even know what the traffic is like, even if it's Sunday? By the time you drop off your bags and get back it'll be 6:30 p.m. We'll meet at 7:30 p.m.' She smiled at the other end. She was thrilled to have him in Bangalore. She had been going through a rough patch, having broken up with her boyfriend a year ago, while Prayas was in the US for a year.

Prayas reached Bangalore Central five minutes before the scheduled time. He couldn't control his excitement to see her. He paced around the mall checking shops and displays while waiting for Purvi, who he knew would be late as usual.

A while later, he felt a tap on his shoulder as he stood waiting for her outside the coffee shop. He turned around to be embraced immediately. She wrapped her arms around him and kissed him on his cheek.

'So there you are my big bear,' she said, smiling at him.

'It's 8:15, you said 7:30. I've grown tired walking around the store.'

'Arrey, you know it takes me a while to get ready, don't you?'

'That's true and a while is how many ages?' he said, jibing on the times she's made him wait in the past.

'Yeah right, let's go now. I'm so happy you've moved here.'

'Where are we going?'

'To Hint, it's a lounge. Let's grab a drink or two. We can go for dinner afterwards.'

'Great,' he said as he followed her up the escalator.

He twisted and turned, while trying to sleep. He remembered how happy the first day in Bangalore had been. The moments he had spent with her had been the happiest of his life. The two years in college and the eight months in Bangalore were what he could trade the rest of his life for. And now she was getting married to someone else.

Why not me? Everything will change now, he realised. She was too good for me anyway.

Elsewhere

In Bangalore

Purvi locked her door and turned off the lights. She didn't want her parents to disturb her anymore. There had been incessant phone calls from her relatives all over the globe, calling to congratulate the family. Hooray! she thought, with a frown on her face. Her soon-to-be husband also called, and wanted to get to know his bride-to-be.

She had curtly told him that it was a little too late to talk, and hung up after some polite banter.

It's all too much, it's such a big deal, she realised. And Prayas is acting daft on the phone. Who does he think he is? He seemed like he didn't care, beyond his 'Are you happy?' and 'Are you sure?' questions.

She lay in bed feeling miserable about her day, and the overwhelming excitement of it all. Most of all she felt alone. Everyone else around her was over the moon, except her.

She got out of bed and opened her wardrobe taking out a bunch of albums. She noticed a grey sweater behind the albums. One that Prayas had gifted her on her last birthday. She held it close to her chest and started to cry.

Five months ago
In Bangalore

As Purvi walked into Corner House Ice Creams, Prayas was sitting there patiently in a blue-white check shirt. She noticed that he had made the effort to dress up and look good today.

'Happy Birthday bossy,' he said, before hugging her and kissing her cheek.

'Thanks! So where's my gift?' she said with a gleam in her eyes.

'Here, sorry I didn't have time to get it packed,' he said, handing her a United Colours of Benetton bag.

'What's this?' she said taking out a grey full sleeves sweater. She bit her lips and then laughed at him. 'What made you pick this up?'

'Why... you don't like it? I saw you pick it up and spend a lot of time looking at it last week, when we went shopping.' He looked worried, while she looked at him seriously, and laughed again.

'Was looking at it for my Mum you fool!'

'Aaah, give it to me, I'll exchange it.'

'No, I like it, I'm keeping it.' She brushed it against her cheek. 'It's soft, thank you.'

'I've ordered your apple pie with whipped cream.'

'You got that right, didn't you?' she said, adjusting her glasses.

'Yes ma'am.'

'Did you pick up the tickets for the movie at Inox?'

'Yes, it's at 7:30 p.m.'

'Good, I have to be home by 11 p.m.'

'You will be, don't worry. I'll drop you back home after the movie.'

'Great! So this is what I get huh? A grey sweater, some yummy apple pie and company to watch a chick flick.' She smiled at him with a glitter in her eyes.

'Yes....I guess; pretty much,' Prayas said hesitantly. He dug his fingers in the pocket of his jeans, and looked at her intently with nervousness in his eyes.

'Stop looking so nervous, you're sweet,' she said, before leaning in and kissing him on his cheek. 'Let's go.'

She got up to try on the sweater. She had never tried it on until now. Her phone started to vibrate. It was 5.00 a.m. She had been up pretty much all night.

It is 5.00 a.m. Does he want to say sorry now? Why didn't he call back earlier? Let it ring, after all he kept me up all night.

She received a message saying, 'pick up'. And the phone started to vibrate again. 'What do you want?' she asked, sounding upset.

'Are you mad at me?'

'Get to the point.' She wiped her tears with the sleeves of her sweater.

'Come downstairs, now.'

'What? Stop kidding me.' She stood up, and brushed her locks behind her ears.

'Come to your window, you'll see a black Aveo, I rented it at the airport. Now come down... I went to the airport, got on a low cost airline, flew all the way here, and drove from the airport the least you can do...'

'Okay don't get cranky, I'm coming.'

'Fast, you don't need make up.'

'Okay,' she said, while putting on a pair of jeans, and tip toeing out of the room.

She was sitting next to him in the car within a few minutes.

'I brought you something. They've opened outside the new airport.' He handed her a little box.

'Apple pie! Wow, thanks, I'll have it for breakfast. You didn't have to fly all the way....'

'Wait, let me talk.'

'Okay.'

'Will you marry me instead?' He looked at her with intensity in his eyes.

'What?'

'I meant to ask you on your birthday. I bought this ring back then. I felt yaar, chod! She's too good for me. That you always will be, but I don't want to lose you PV, I love you.'

'Yes, yes I will.' She put her arms around his neck and kissed him on his forehead and then his lips.

She stared at the ring on her finger. 'What took you so long, you big clown?'

'You intimidate me, I get scared.'

'I know,' she smiled, and pulled his cheek.

'I can see you're wearing the grey sweater.'

'He he, yes, I am. It looks really nice, hai na?' She blushed, and locked her gaze with his.

'Go pack some clothes, leave a little note. Let's get hitched and come back in a few days. I've booked us on the 9.00 a.m. flight back to Pune.'

'Okay, I'll be back in ten minutes,' she said before getting out of the car, and walking towards her house.

He watched her slender figure, accentuated by the tight fitting grey sweater disappear behind the gate as he took a bite from her half-eaten apple pie. He smiled to himself dreaming about his life ahead with the girl in the grey sweater, his best friend and the woman of his dreams.

•➤

Love-all

KUNAL DHABALIA

'Can you pass me the salt?' I heard the question but did not pay any attention to it, until the same voice repeated, 'Excuse me, can you pass the salt?'

This time I did realize that the voice was directed at me and the girl to whom it belonged was sitting on the same table as I was, separated by two empty chairs. 'I'm sorry, but I was preoccupied,' I said, apologizing, as I passed the salt.

'It's Okay, I understand. Didn't you join Colosseum Corp just today?'

I had joined Colosseum Corp that morning and wondered how she knew this. For the first time I looked at her properly—a white shirt, short hair, a pair of glasses perched on her head, and a shy smile, looking more like a college student than an office-goer—and inquired, 'How do you know?'

'Don't you remember me?' she asked.

Ah, the favourite and most (ab)used pickup line of the universe.

But wait a second, I've never heard a girl use this line before; leave alone this line, no girl has ever used any pickup line on me.

It has always been me who falls hook, line and sinker in love with every girl. So it did seem that she genuinely knew me. I tried to place her, racked my brains, but came up with nothing. Cursing myself for not remembering such a beautiful face, I said, 'I'm sorry, I don't remember you'

'Come on, you kept flirting with me and now you don't even remember me,' she said.

I have always been a flirt. Anytime I see a beautiful girl, I can't help myself. It is as if I gain a new personality at such times. Being a serial flirt and blessed with an exceptional ability to not remember people's faces I had faced this situation scores of times and was having difficulty remembering when and where I had hit on her.

Seeing that I was unable to place her, she said, 'I am offended.' Before I could apologize, a guy materialized in the chair opposite hers, 'Sorry Ragini, got stuck in a meeting.'

'Ragini'—I knew that name. While I was pathetic with faces, I was very good with names. The only Ragini I knew was the one who took my HR round of interview for Colosseum Corp. And I recalled I had flirted with her shamelessly. I had been smitten with her ever since she had received me at Colosseum Corp for my interviews and had guided me through the maze of cubicles. Once all my technical interviews had been over, she called me in for the HR interview and I even opened the door to her office for her. Not just chivalrous, I had been hilarious that day. I remembered it was more like two friends talking rather than an interview.

How can a girl look so different by just changing her hair style?

Leave alone her, I could not even recognize Bollywood actresses if they altered their look a bit. If a heroine sports short hair after having long tresses for a long time, I can never recognize her. How in God's name do people recognize each other after so many years surely beats me. I thought of explaining all this to Ragini, but was reluctant to say anything in front of her companion.

Second day at Colosseum Corp: time for my orientation programme. In layman's terms, I was being potty-trained—being told how to behave, whom to talk to, whom not to talk to. In sum, I was being told to be a good boy. What made this torture slightly endurable was that Ragini was the one taking the orientation.

What made the class less interesting was that the guy from lunch table kept interrupting Ragini's melodious voice with his croaks.

Finally, the session ended. I coughed up enough courage to walk up to her and apologize, 'I am so sorry about yesterday. I am bad at identifying faces and this is not the first time I have been in trouble because of this.'

She smiled. 'Oh it's okay. It was fun seeing you in so much confusion and discomfort.'

Before I could say anything Croaky interrupted us. 'Ragini coming for lunch?'

She nodded and turned to me. 'Joining us?'

'Sure,' I said and followed them to the cafeteria.

As we started lunch, Ragini introduced Croaky to me. 'This is Neeraj, my boyfriend.' It was a weird way to introduce a co-worker to a newbie in the company, but then it could have been an attempt to dissuade me from hitting on her.

Turning to Croaky, she said, 'And this is Sid, remember the guy who kept flirting with me while I was interviewing him? That surely was a memorable experience.'

I expected Croaky to be pissed off, instead he was cool. 'Dude, you have become a legend in the Human Resources Department. Nobody has done anything remotely as insane as what you did— hitting on your interviewer.'

'Well now that you mention it in such terms, Neeraj,' I said,

'I am surprised I got the offer.'

'Oh that was because you were very good in your other interviews and you definitely are an avant-garde charmer,' Ragini chimed in.

My thought bubble read, 'Ah! So, the charms worked on you. Want to see if they work a second time over coffee?' But I uttered nothing, as Ragini would have guessed I was hitting on her again and pre-empt all my moves. Anyway, I would not gain anything by hitting on her. One, she is already in a relationship. Two, it is a bad idea to invite the ire of an HR personnel. So I simply said, 'Thanks', and moved the conversation to safer topics.

It had been a draining day; the technical trainings had been a bit too technical for my taste. I never did like any acronyms, and here everything hinged on acronyms. My brain buzzing with arcane acronyms, I filled my lunch plate, and was heading to the last table when I heard a 'Hey!' Recognizing the voice, I turned to see Neeraj beckoning me to join him and Ragini for lunch. As I neared the table, I caught a snippet of conversation—Neeraj was saying, '... boring. Reminds me of the ketchup ad.' I fired an arrow in the dark, 'Come on Neeraj, how can you say that about tennis? The Federer-Nadal rivalry is stuff worthy of legends.'

They turned towards me and judging by their looks, the arrow seemed to have hit bullseye. Ragini recovered first, 'Whoa Sid! You don't look like a telepathic. And Neeraj, he is absolutely right—tennis is seeing one of the greatest rivalries of all times.'

Neeraj scoffed, 'Save your tennis talks for each other. And don't bore me.'

We did bore him as Ragini and I kept talking about tennis and tried to brainwash Neeraj into following tennis.

That day on, I joined Ragini and Neeraj for lunch daily, and became very good friends with both. Soon our talks spilled over the work hours. As I was new to Hyderabad, Neeraj and Ragini took it on themselves to show me around. Within a few days the famous Hyderabadi Biryani became our staple diet.

To me they were the ideal couple. At times their connection seemed to be telepathic. She was perfect, and he—although not perfect (how can a guy be perfect if he does not like tennis?)—was awesome. I was the kabab-me-haddi, but I never felt so. Actually, I think Neeraj felt more like a third wheel whenever Ragini and I started talking about tennis, which was often. She was a Nadal fan, and I was a Federer fanatic and we would spend hours discussing the merits and demerits of their playing styles.

I had settled nicely in my job and in Hyderabad, and had made two life-long friends when life turned upside down. Ragini told me suddenly that Neeraj and she were breaking up. To say that it came as a shock would be an understatement. I pictured them as a perfect couple who were always happy, and an issue like a break-up was not even on the horizon. It turned out that they wanted to get married, but the typical issue of caste reared its ugly head again. Ragini was an Iyer, Neeraj a Marwari, and their parents, being from small towns in Tamil Nadu and Rajasthan respectively, were staunchly against the marriage. Neeraj had suggested eloping, but Ragini was vehemently against it. Soon this issue escalated, and unable to find a resolution they decided to break-up.

I spent the next few days in shock. I'd have lunch one day with Ragini, the other day with Neeraj, but all the lunches were spent the same way—staring silently at the plate and playing around with the food. Neeraj went ahead and moved to another team, so that they both would be spared the discomfort of working together. Since Neeraj moved to another building, I spent all my time with Ragini. After a few days, she began opening up, and told me about her ultra-conservative family where even a love-marriage was looked down on and marrying outside the caste was considered blasphemy. On my part, I tried to keep her as happy as possible. There was a tennis tournament happening in Hyderabad, and even though there were no big names playing, I took her to the Lal Bahadur Stadium to rekindle her love for tennis. The ploy seemed to work, as soon I found myself signing up for a tennis training academy at Ragini's insistence. She threw herself into the game. Her enthusiasm for tennis was incredible and infectious, and soon I had to train harder as she wanted to take part in a mixed-doubles tournament.

As I kept spending more and more time with Ragini, I found myself thinking about her constantly. I felt happy when at the tennis academy, and at the mixed-doubles tournament, we were mistaken for a couple. True, the first time I met her I had been a flirt and had hit on her, but I had changed. We had been great friends for a year now. But since her break-up, I had become her emotional support as well, and I felt nice being the one who took care of her. She ruled my thoughts—day and night. I wanted to know what she felt too, but how could I ask her? I could not date her—dating works for people who don't know each other. But Ragini and I knew each other a bit too well. I knew that she was not the same Ragini post break- up. She had lost an irreplaceable part of her life, and she knew that nobody else would understand her as well as I did. We were compatible with each other, we were comfortable in each others' silences, we had an intuitive connection on the tennis court, and I knew for sure we would be perfect for each other. But how could I ask her, how could I risk our entire friendship?

The confusion had been going on for a few weeks, when one day I bumped into Neeraj. He had left the company soon after the break-up and although we kept in touch via emails, it was not the same as the drunken nights we three used to spend before their break-up. Just as Ragini had thrown herself into tennis, Neeraj had thrown himself into his work, and was climbing the corporate ladder at a scary pace.

They had not talked to each other for a year now, and even then Neeraj's first question was, 'How is Ragini?'

'She is doing good. She turned professional at tennis last month,' I replied.

'Awesome, I hope she has modelled her game on Nadal's. I used to hate that guy—the way he kept interrupting our conversations with his awesome winners.'

'She modelled her game copying Federer,' I said.

'Hmm, yeah I guess Nadal's power game would not be her cup of tea.'

Neeraj and tennis? I was surprised, 'How come you are talking about tennis?'

Neeraj said, 'Well, you know how after a break-up, you miss all the small caring things that the other half did for you?' As I shrugged, he continued, 'Surprisingly what I missed the most were her incoherent tennis talks. Somehow I too was bitten by the tennis bug and started following it.'

We talked for some more time about Ragini, before going our respective ways.

The next day I met Ragini, and told her about meeting Neeraj. Immediately I was besieged with questions—how was he, how did he look, did he ask about her, did he look happy and a million other questions. As I kept answering her questions, Ragini's face got a different glow. When I told her that Neeraj had started following tennis, she laughed uproariously. I had not heard her laugh this way in the last year. That minute I knew that even now I was the fly in the soup. There was no Ragini and me. It had always been Ragini and Neeraj. I knew I had to play Cupid.

Ragini was playing a local tennis tournament, and without her knowledge I invited Neeraj. Neeraj thought I was taking him for an IPL match, but instead I drove him to the tennis court. Neeraj realized my plan and was surprisingly eager to see Ragini. I had thought I would have to force the both of them to talk out their issues. My work seemed to be getting easier. Ragini waved a hello to me as I entered the court, and her wave stopped midway when she recognized the person following me. She immediately became nervous, and got off to a bad start. Her game did not improve and within an hour she had lost the match.

After an awkward 'Hi' and 'Hello', I left them alone to sort out their issues. Two hours later, I received a call and an exhilarated Ragini said, 'We are back together. We'll convince our parents somehow.'

I had expected I would be a tad disappointed on hearing this, but I surprised myself—I was overjoyed. 'Congratulations!' I said.

'We owe it to you Sid, thanks a lot.'

Even today Ragini blames me for her losing that match, but she still thanks me for the same.

·◆

Moving On

AHMED FAIYAZ

Saira walked into Ajay's room. The drapes were drawn and she saw him lying in bed, staring blankly at the plain white ceiling.

'Hey! Why are you so glum, Ajay?' she asked, before sitting on the bed next to him. Ajay was her childhood friend and they had been together in school and college. He had gone to London, for a Masters in Political Science, eight months ago, and was back in Hyderabad for his winter break.

'You know why…' he said, looking sullen and withdrawn.

'Oh come on! Get over it Ajay! It's been a couple of months already. Sitting and sulking won't help in sorting things out between Kirti and you.'

'How could she, Saira? We were together for three years! I leave for London and a few months later she starts seeing that fool of a credit card salesman…' he said with some annoyance.

'He's the Divisional Sales Manager of the Credit Cards Business at the Bank of Singapore…'

'Whose side are you on?'

'Dude, get real! You dated Kirti… you know how she is! She's spoilt and she needs a lot of attention. You went away and she found a "Mr Right Now", Saira said, pushing behind her curly auburn hair.

'We were in love! How could she just walk out on a serious and committed relationship? Besides, she began seeing him while we were still together.'

'Right, like when you guys spoke on the phone once in a couple of days. Yaar, you were in a long-distance relationship, and it didn't work. It wasn't going to, given the person Kirti Rao is, so deal with it…'

'Do you think she'll take me back?' he asked looking at her with desperation in his eyes.

'What? Are you nuts?' Saira was flabbergasted. She walked across the room, and looked at her reflection in the mirror. 'Do you think I've put on weight?'

'No, you look great. That dress looks really nice on you.' She smiled, and blushed. She realised that she had packed a few pounds since she began working as the Accounts Manager at Raju Labs.

'But seriously, I still can't believe what Kirti did to me. Why don't you talk some sense into her Saira? Both of you have been friends,' he said softly.

'No way! She knows I'm more your friend than hers. I don't want to be taking sides and spoiling my friendship with her. I told her what I had to, months ago. She chose to do what she did. You should chill, really. In the end she's going to get hitched to someone her family picks for her. Some US-educated doctor or engineer.'

'But I'm in love with her…' he said looking distressed.

'Why don't you get ready lover boy? It's Nishant's birthday party at Ahala. The gang is meeting us there in half-hour.'

'I'm not in the mood. You should go ahead if you want to. Kirti's going to be there. I'm sure that moron will tag along with a smirk on his face.'

'Stop being a baby. You're like twenty-three! You have to grin and deal with it. Nishant and you have been friends for a long time. Besides, I didn't drive all the way from Basheerbagh to Jubilee Hills to sit here and listen to you mourn about Kirti. I've heard a lot already. You cribbed about this the whole time, the day we went for coffee to Barista, and then again yesterday, when we went to pick up books from Walden.

'You can understand my position right? I mean after all I've done...'

'I can baba. You're right, Kirti has been cruel. This is how the world is! Now will you please get ready in ten minutes?'

'Do I have a choice?' he asked with a frown on his face.

'Not really,' she said with an impish grin.

An hour later they were inside the club, along with a group of their old friends. House music played in the background with a number of people letting their hair loose on the dance floor, as the tequila shots flowed.

'Let's leave in an hour,' Ajay said, while sipping on his whisky and coke.

'Why? We've only just got here. Besides, Kirti is away on the dance floor. Can't you look at someone else...' she said, turning her gaze to meet his.

'Look at the way he's putting his arms around her, that damn wolf! What does she see in him? His unshaven scruffy looks, shabby sense of dressing....he doesn't even work out! I mean what do they talk about? She grew up in Banjara Hills and he's a Guntur boy! How the hell does that fit? Look at the way he's dancing!'

'He's got a good job, drives a nice car and does enough to show her a good time. All of what you said doesn't even matter...' Saira smiled wryly, 'She isn't looking to marry him.'

'It's disgusting,' Ajay said, quickly downing his glass of whisky and gesturing at the bartender to serve him one more.

'It's life Ajay,' Saira said, while sipping on her mocktail. 'You're a nice guy; you can do a lot better. Who is Kirti beyond a pencil-thin figure and a great pair of legs? She's a shallow person, quite dull-headed in my opinion.'

'I thought she was your friend,' he said with a bitter laugh.

'She is, but that doesn't change my opinion about her. You're not in love with her. It's about your ego being hurt.'

'It's not that…'

'Of course it is…he isn't as good-looking or as smart as you, yet there he is, a small-town bloke, with his arms around your ex-girlfriend.'

'Okay, forget it, I don't really care. To hell with both of them! He can go and max out his credit card entertaining her for all I care,' he said, smiling to himself, while she looked at him teasingly.

'You're a sweetheart! Why didn't I fall in love with you instead of Kirti?'

'Yeah, why didn't you?' she asked with a glitter in her eyes. In that moment, he found himself drawn towards her. Her soft pink lips, her fragrance, her delicate curvy frame and her baby-face struck him suddenly. It was like he had been blind to how beautiful Saira was.

Back in London he missed her the most and longed to speak to her.

'Well, I don't know. My bad luck I guess…' he said taking his gaze away from hers. 'What's happening with that chap, Shakir? He has a soft-spot for you, doesn't he?'

'Uff, don't start! Thank god his incessant calls have reduced. He asks me out like two-three times a week. He simply doesn't get it. I'm not interested.'

'He's a nice guy. I think he really likes you,' Ajay said earnestly.

'Well, I'm not sure if it makes any sense, I don't see the

chemistry between us.'

'Dude, meet Sarika.' Nishant butted in, 'She's my cousin from Chennai and she's moving to London this fall for a course in advertising. Sarika, this is my buddy Ajay, and with him is the elusive Saira. We get to see her only when Ajay is in town,' Nishant said with a laugh. Sarika said hi, her gaze set on Ajay.

'Shut up, Nishant! I have a job, unlike some spoilt people who join the family business,' Saira quipped.

'Hey, I work too. Maybe I have it a little easier than you do,' Nishant shrugged good-naturedly, 'Anyway, Ajay, maybe you can help Sarika out… help her settle in? She doesn't really know many people out there.'

Ajay glanced in her direction with interest while she gazed at him with a demure smile. He liked what he saw. She wasn't fair like Saira, nor did she have Kirti's sharp features, but he found her very attractive. She was tall and dusky, with a nose ring, a tattoo on her arm and a devil-may-care attitude about her. He thought that she was one of the sexiest women in the club, with streaks of blonde in her hair and tanned legs.

'It'll be great to have someone I know out there,' she said with a smile in her husky voice while Nishant moved next to Saira to catch up with her.

A few minutes later, Ajay and Sarika moved over to the dance floor where they showed off some salsa steps. Both of them were clearly trained dancers. Even Kirti stopped to gape at Ajay with wonder. She preferred the image of heartbroken lover over the hot-stepper she was seeing on the dance floor.

Saira ordered another mocktail and watched the two couples on the dance floor with interest.

'Do you want to dance?' Nishant asked. 'Come on Saira, it'll be fun!'

'No, please. I'm not much of a dancer really! I'd rather sit here and enjoy the music,' she said, as she watched Ajay match steps with Sarika. She did like to dance but didn't feel like it.

Twenty minutes later, Ajay came over to the bar to get Sarika a drink. Saira was sitting there with Nishant and a couple of other friends.

'Do you want to leave Ajay? It's past one and I need to get to work tomorrow,' she said, moving close to him.

'Hey, sorry babe! I'm going to stay a bit. We're having a good time,' he said flashing a smile towards the dance floor, 'I'll take a cab back or hitch a ride with Sarika if she's driving.'

'Okay, I'll take off then. You take it easy with the drinks alright? You're high already.'

He leaned forward and kissed her on her cheek before hugging her. 'You're a doll, always looking out for me. Thanks for bringing me out here... Sarika is something else! I'll speak to you later. Get home safely,' he said before turning away and picking up Sarika's drink from the bar.

'I will,' she mumbled with a forced smile before turning back to the group she had been chatting with. She said her goodbyes and walked out of the club thinking, I wish he realised how I feel about him. He just doesn't get it... Maybe he will some day.

The next evening

Saira walked into her room to take a shower and get dressed. She had a dinner planned with Ajay at Ohri's, one of their old favourites, as he was set to leave for London in a couple of days. Her phone rang.

'Hi, give me fifteen minutes and I'll be ready,' she said hurriedly.

I'll wear that black dress, that'll surprise him. He hasn't seen me in such an avatar.

'Hey, actually I was... err...wondering if we could do a rain check on tonight?' Ajay's voice wheedled, 'Thing is that Sarika goes back to Chennai tomorrow and she wanted to head out tonight...'

'But Ajay, I left early from work and....'

'Sorry baba! I'll make it up to you. Let's do brunch on Sunday. I don't leave till late on Sunday night.'

'Fine, I'll call you tomorrow.' She hung up and walked into the restroom. She slumped down with her back against the wall and broke down.

A few minutes later, she heard a knock on the door. It was her mother. Saira quickly wiped her tears, and opened the door.

'Saira beti, what happened? Why are you crying? Did you have a fight with Ajay?' Her nose was red, and so were her moist eyes.

She stayed silent for a minute but the recent disappointment was too fresh and she broke down again in her mother's arms. They sat down on her bed and Saira poured her heart out. She shared how deeply she felt for Ajay but he never noticed. He couldn't see how much she loved him and always took her for granted.

'Beti, I've always let you live your life your way. It's a luxury that I didn't have while growing up. But don't depress yourself like this. You're too young....You've been blessed, you're a nice-looking girl.'

'Ammi,' she said, 'but why can't he realise?'

'Forget that. Just get up from here and go wash your face. Then put on your best dress... We'll go out for dinner, just you and I. Call Shakir, that boy has called twice asking for you. And stop killing yourself over someone who's probably having a good time somewhere.'

Her mother walked out of the room leaving Saira to ponder over the comments she had just made.

She called Shakir, 'Hi, sorry I missed your call. Tell me.'

'Hi Saira, I'm so glad you called. Indian Ocean is playing at

Secunderabad Club tomorrow night. I've got passes. Do you want to go? It'll be fun.'

'I'm not sure Shakir. Tomorrow's Saturday, and it's possible that I'll be working till half-past-seven.'

'Oh okay... well if you want, you can take these passes and go with someone else too.' There was a moment of silence.

'Actually, let's go, it won't start before 10.00 p.m. anyway. Come and pick me up by 9.'

'Wonderful! I'll see you tomorrow, don't change your mind.'

'I won't,' she said with a laugh and hung up. Let me keep this black dress away for tomorrow, she thought, putting it away in her wardrobe and pulling out a stylish red salwar dress.

Two years later

'You look beautiful,' Ajay said looking at Saira with affection. 'I wish I'd known how hot you would look as a bride. You have been starving for months to lose all that baby fat, haven't you?'

'Ajay, behave! Don't make fun of me,' she said sweetly. She wore a blue and gold wedding dress adorned with jewels and a diamond pendant around her neck.

'So, are you all set?' he asked with a wry smile.

'Do you think it's the right thing to do? I mean this isn't about Shakir, but marriage is a big deal. You know better,' Saira hesitated, 'you've been divorced and it was rough. Is marriage worth it?' she asked with searching eyes.

He turned his gaze away from her. 'I think it is. Shakir is devoted towards you. He worships the ground you walk on... he has from day one. He's had eyes only for you.'

It brought a bright smile back to her face and a dreamy look in her eyes. 'Yes he has and I love him,' she gushed. 'He's been very nice with the family too. My parents can be quite overbearing at times.'

'Saira beti, come on. Everyone is waiting, it's time to go,' her mother called out, while her giggling cousin sisters walked into the room.

'Haan Ammi,' she said, before getting up and walking out of the room, while Ajay gave her a thumbs up sign, and followed her out. He was lost in his thoughts and deep down, he felt crushed. He wondered what could have been between Saira and him. *I wish she knew, I was foolish and I took too long to realise how I felt about her. I moved from one stupid fling to another. Maybe I should have told her a few moments ago.*

He got into his car to follow the car that was taking the bride and her parents to Taj Banjara for the nikah and the reception. He reflected on why his marriage to Sarika had fallen apart. Through it, he was always thinking *what if?* It was as if he was looking for Saira in his now estranged wife.

He jogged his memory back to four weeks ago when Saira had called him in Delhi to say that she was getting married to Shakir. He hadn't known how to react then and he didn't know what to do now.

'Oh Saira, I wish you knew how much I love you. What am I supposed to do?' he muttered to himself, as he drove out from her building. *Why can't she realise how I feel about her?*

•◆

The Untouched Guitar

SAHIL KHAN

Seems this Moleskine is going to be wasted with scratched out notes. Line after line, verse after verse— Zoeb still can't make sense of it. Precious as it may be to me, there's something more important which he needs to pen down.

Three years ago, while in college, I met Zoeb. The seniors were ragging him and a few of them had noticed me. I was the next bali ka bakra. Zoeb had been caught with a guitar and had just finished some song and soon I was singing with him playing along some random chords. Poor chap.

An hour had passed since we had bravely presented ourselves on the platter to the seniors and many more had been made to stand on the prestigious podium. Meanwhile, I had noticed Zoeb exchanging glances with her, a senior. Aah, the taste he had for pretty women coupled with functional grey matter. A month later, they were dating.

But today, he's trying to make up for one of the many things she says he botched up.

He loved her like crazy; still does. Worked his charm, but seems it didn't last long. Wit and humour did fail him, finally. I had told him, many times, think about now.

He didn't pray, yet he had faith. Life may have screwed him over, yet life is his Holy Grail.

I'd die for a girl like her, and I suppose most of the guys around did. But here she was—Zoeb's girl. She had dated a batch-mate in her first year which hadn't worked out. And now she's with Zoeb—her junior and my roommate.

Being my roomie, he'd tell me what's going on in his life—about her, about other stuff. His band had been practicing hard and was getting a few gigs around town. She never accompanied him for the gigs. The band would get back and Zoeb would celebrate the gig with her; mostly with chicken tandoori and a bottle of wine. I'd usually take a glass from them, and disappear into my room to watch a movie I had just finished downloading. God, I love torrents!

He had a way with words. I had seen some of his writing apart from the songs for the band and I'm surprised he wasn't freelancing already. Maybe someday he would. He'd tell me of the times when he'd pick up the guitar when she was around and he'd churn out random lyrics, making her laugh. Pulling words out of thin air alongside a peppy chord progression, Zoeb could set the most ill-disposed person to a rather cheery mood. He had shown her all his writings from the school days to present. We three had shared a few laughs on the wannabe rebellious lyrics that he had jotted down in two notebooks. Stuff like 'with the acid dripping, burn by burn; with the heart resounding, echo by echo'—hilarious!

Zoeb got influenced a lot by what he saw, read and heard. A song by a Pakistani singer, whom he's not a big fan of these days, inspired him to write his first song in Urdu. That song still resonates in the minds of people who've heard it. He had written it for a girl he had a thing for back in school. Since then, Zoeb's hardly written a song in English. He finds Urdu to be more heart-warming.

With each passing day, Zoeb's need to be different was taking him down new roads. He had always cribbed about the college not having a student's magazine. He had even tried speaking to the management and a few people about it but for some reason it didn't materialize. Fed up, he went ahead to setup his own magazine.

He'd now spend lesser time jamming with his band and more time at seminars, conferences, networking events, college events, scouting for possible writers, fishing for money, gathering feedback. He'd come back and discuss the magazine with her and me. It was all that he could talk about. He'd buy magazines and jot down what he liked about each issue—the topics, the writing style, the design and layout, the pictures. He would spend hours on the web reading blogs on understanding trends, what journalists have to say about new media and the sorts. He took up assignments at various publications just to understand how they worked. Money didn't concern him yet.

Six months on, he had a team of eight people helping him sift through the content that was flowing in. Two of them were design students who helped him in the layouts. I wonder why he had taken up a fortnightly issue. He had converted the hall of our 2BHK into the magazine's office. People shuffled in and out through the hours. I didn't complain. Instead, it made me want to work and I did help Zoeb once in a while with some decisions since I had come to know him well as a person as we were staying together.

It was nice to see her accompany Zoeb to events, take interviews and share some of his responsibilities. I could see Zoeb pouring his heart and soul to this project, and I could see her being neglected slightly. I assumed she understood Zoeb's priorities regarding the magazine, but it seems I was wrong. Guess I should've been more explicit with the think-of-the-now talk that I had given him a couple of times.

Earlier Zoeb had seemed uninterested in college and he rarely attended lectures. But now he liked attending them and I could see why. He now understood certain things better than most because of the magazine he had been running. I saw him running against time, trying to pack in as many things as possible in the twenty-four hours he had. He'd spend the entire day neck-deep in work, while she'd spend the entire day waiting for his call.

Things were changing. She was soon going to graduate. She would pack her bags and head back to her parents. I could feel the pressure of time closing on them. In an effort to make the relationship work, they were trying to make last-minute compromises. I knew of enough relationships that had been ruined by the distance. God forbid, I wouldn't want this relationship to fall apart. But isn't this how most college relationships end anyway?

It's now been almost a year since she finished college. I am prepping up for stepping into the corporate world. College placement has got me a decent job, but I might leave it and join a start-up. Living with Zoeb has made me realize that responsibility was more important than the money. My parents hate him for that.

Zoeb is still devoted to the magazine and plans to expand his team.

She had come down a couple of times to meet Zoeb and spend some time together. He had taken the train many a times to go meet her. He'd always carry his laptop bundled with a USB modem so that he could work, even when she was over at his hotel room. She understood and adjusted, but seems there's always a limit. They took a break a month ago.

She laid down everything that troubled her regarding the relationship. That first song in Hindi had come back to bite him in the ass. He's performed that song at various gigs to much applause, and apparently she's miffed about not having a song being written for her. Girls these days, sigh!

In the past one month, they tried sorting things out; one by one.

From that day until now, Zoeb's been trying to write her a song. He told me that he had tried earlier as well, when their relationship was in the pink of health, but he had ended up scraping the paper. He said, he hadn't been able to do her justice. The moron should've understood that she would've loved anything he had written for her.

But again, you never know girls. What if she had created a ruckus for it not being better than that first song?

Three years. It was three years ago, while in college, I had met Zoeb and I had seen him exchanging glances with her. And now, three years later, I was soon going to say good-bye to him, and just hope that he could work his charm with her all over again. Fingers crossed.

He flips the Moleskine away and goes in to his room. He's given up? What did he spend the last few hours writing? I take a look.

Ae Khuda, tu yeh bata
Waqt jo, tune guzaara;
Maula mere, kaise karun mein
Barhayi in alfazon se.

He couldn't put a tune to this to save his ass? Dumb f***!

◆

Between Friends

PARITOSH UTTAM

There was desolation all around
until you became my friend
the best companion I ever found
on the journey to life's end
said the Hallmark card. Mushy, sing-song, pretentious.

For someone who brings Hope to Life,
For someone who stands by us till Eternity,
For someone who is a True Friend
said the Archies one. Impersonal, clichéd, too many capitals.

Siddartha moved out of the greeting cards section and saw the little heart-shaped plaque of red velvet with silver lettering across it: I found a friend in you. He got it gift-wrapped and taped a card on it addressed 'To Dear Sanjana'.

Dear Sanjana, he found as expected, sitting alone at the table at the farthest end from the entrance to the cafeteria. The cafeteria was one place in the Pune University campus that was never empty, unlike the college library or the gymkhana, until it closed late in the night. Siddhartha strode up to her table, pulled a chair and sat facing her.

'Knew you would be here.'

'Where else you know you can always find me here.' She spoke, with the same lack of punctuation that she practised in her emails. She did not seem surprised by his arrival. Her voice, husky, sounded as though she suffered from a perennial sore throat. But it went along with the rest of her appearance, as if The Maker, in giving her a masculine frame, wanted to go the whole stretch. Indeed, if she had a soft, girlish voice, it would have been all the more incongruous.

'Well, happy birthday,' Siddhartha said, holding out his hand to shake hers. She accepted his wishes, again without showing any surprise at his remembering, although he could see she was pleased. He then took out the gift-wrapped box from his pocket, rearranged the card and placed it before her. This evoked some reaction.

'Oh wow thanks can I open it here.' The wrapper was in her hands before he could reply.

'Thanks Sid it is sweet,' she said, holding the plaque in her hand. He knew she meant it and felt pleased because she was.

He looked at the tables behind, worried that someone might be watching them. From a distance, one would see only a red heart and not the wordings on it, and the implication could be embarrassing. Siddhartha let out a silent sigh of relief as thankfully, no one was looking their way.

Would he really feel embarrassed if the campus grapevine carried rumours linking Sanjana and him romantically? Perhaps not. Rather, it would be funny. Of all the girls in the college, his friends would mock, Sid could not find anybody other than Sanju baba. But she had a heart of gold. What had happened with Ankita?

Barbie doll-like plastic beauty with as much plastic in her heart. She had not wasted much time in moving on to Akshay only because his father was rich enough to gift him his own car. Siddhartha could not imagine her losing any sleep over ditching him. Her last words to him, weeks ago, had been, 'Let's remain friends, Sid?' Of course there was no inverse relation between a girl's beauty and nature, but one example of either case in one's life—Ankita: beautiful but cruel; Sanjana: plain but kind-hearted—went a long way in establishing a hypothesis.

Sanjana sat hunched forward, elbows resting on the table, blowing and creating a mini-whirlpool in the cup of coffee between them. The arms of her denim jacket were folded back at the cuffs, revealing wrists a tennis player would have been proud of. Her hair barely reached her shoulders, and at the front they hung straight down like the frayed edge of a curtain, framing her face. Siddartha saw with a start that something in her face had altered. The eyebrows. She had got them shaped, apparently deciding that they did not have to be thick, bushy ones that met over the bridge of her nose.

Siddhartha decided that it would take much more than shaped-eyebrows to make her look good, or that he had simply got used to her earlier appearance. But he was touched. For never before had she shown the slightest concern about her looks, and now it seemed as if the woman in her had at last decided to wake up from its dormancy.

'Something on your mind what are you thinking,' she asked.

'Nothing,' he said quickly, laughing to himself. That was Sanjana. Sometimes he feared she could read his thoughts, when he thought she was not even looking.

'Is it Ankita when will you forget her.'

'No, no. Long time since I thought of her.'

'Good.'

She had got it wrong this time; he was not thinking of Ankita at all. What he said was true, well almost true, because one never gets over a first love, especially when it fails. But it had stopped hurting now, and that was what Sanjana wanted to hear.

The tears and the pangs of sorrow and anger were very much there—before he met Sanjana. Despite being sympathetic, none of his friends were able to comfort him. A pat on the back with the words, 'It happens to everyone, dude. Move on,' were indicative of their support but did not provide solace. And a twenty-year old guy in college cannot weep on the shoulders of other twenty-year old guys.

One needs feminine shoulders for that, and the broad ones of Sanjana, though no less masculine in appearance, had come to his aid. He remembered quite clearly, soon after his break-up, coming to the cafeteria for lunch alone, unable to join in the usual banter of his classmates, discussing movies and cricket matches. He too did not want to be a damp squib on their conversation. The only vacant table was Sanjana's. Shrugging his shoulders he sat opposite her and ate in silence, a blank stare fixed at his plate.

'Forget her she is not worth it.' The rapid-fire sentence coming from Sanjana, still bent over her plate, startled him. He began to get angry but then imagined the despondent and ridiculous figure he must be making, so obvious to all, that he had to laugh. She looked up with an impish smile and their friendship took off from there.

Their meeting in the cafeteria at lunch and teatime became regular. She was in a different class, so they did not meet in the same lectures, but he soon found he was looking forward to their meetings in the cafeteria. At first he was mocked: of all the girls, Sanju baba! The unkind name, alluding to the macho Bollywood hero Sanjay Dutt, was not without basis. He could not deny her manly girth, her slouching gait and the fact that she was the only girl in college who rode a geared bike, a 150 cc one at that, without even resorting to the electronic start.

After a while, it stopped mattering. And when his friends saw him recovering his earlier cheerfulness and humour, they refrained from teasing him. Sanjana was refreshingly different from the other girls he met. She talked with directness, bereft of any girlish airs or giggly behaviour, but with a sensitivity that was soothingly feminine.

His physique, slighter in comparison to hers, must have made them seem an odd couple. The thought, coming to him while he watched her finish her coffee, surprised him. It was funny to think of themselves as a couple.

'So what's the plan tonight? Where's the birthday party?' he asked.

'No party I am here where would I go.'

'Come on! Not even tonight?'

'No you know I don't go out.'

Siddartha snorted in exasperation. He carried on, failing to notice that her smile had become fixed. 'Don't be silly. Let's go out and have a wonderful dinner. How about Chinese? All Stir Fried at E-Square? Just next door. Expensive, I admit, but we can enjoy one day in a year, right?'

'No thanks Sid I said no.' Even the fixed smile had vanished and this time he didn't miss the seriousness. 'But why?'

'Because I don't go out especially with guys it gives the wrong ideas.' After a pause, unusual for her, she added, 'to others.'

He gaped at her.

'I am sorry you find me old-fashioned,' she said and shrugged, the gesture belying her feeling sorry. 'E-square dinner, movie and so on.'

'But it's me!' he said. 'Not just some guy.'

'I know but…' she shrugged again. 'Sorry.'

Fury writhed inside him like a serpent. He had offered the idea of dinner out of pure friendship and that she should misconstrue it as a cheap overture, was demeaning to him. Maybe his idea was not so pure, maybe there was an element of overture in it, but that she should turn it down mortified him. Coming from her, it was as big an insult as he could imagine.

Had it been Ankita he could have borne it. But Sanjana? The Sanjana who was so manly that the guys mocked her behind her back for never wearing anything other than jeans and shirts; the Sanjana who was so friendless that she had to eat alone— that Sanjana had turned down his harmless offer and was acting unapproachable.

Unapproachable with him whom even Ankita had once found attractive. The wrathful serpent in his heart sat up, ready to strike and spit venom.

'But it's all right to meet here daily? That doesn't give wrong ideas to others?'

Sanjana frowned. 'You crazy or what.'

'Oh yes I am crazy. Meeting here is fine, but going out is wrong. Shaping your eyebrows and waiting for me here, that doesn't give wrong ideas?'

She stared at him. A tear glistened briefly and vanished as suddenly as it had appeared. Her face hardened and smoothed out the creases in her forehead. She got up.

'Look, I didn't mean that—' he began, but she had already pushed her chair back so hard that it fell over with a crash. He could only watch her back receding away from him on the way out.

Outside, a motorbike burst into life and roared away.

Siddartha set the chair back upright and finished his coffee.

Then he too got up and went out slowly. The road was empty. To one side, on the top of a garbage pile, a shiny red plaque caught his eye. He kicked the rubbish over it until it was lost to sight.

•◆

Angst

Just Average

MALATHI JAIKUMAR

There was nothing very exceptional about Shashikala. She was five feet two, the average height for an Indian woman. She was neither dark nor fair, a sort of wheatish complexion. Her features were nondescript. Her eyes were neither large nor beautiful, her nose neither Grecian nor snub, her mouth neither full nor fine. Her saris and salwar kameezes were clean but mostly dull in colour and her hair was always done up in a ponytail or bun. She was not very slim nor was she fat. In fact, she could be described in two words. Just average.

She was not extraordinarily intelligent. She was not passionate about anything nor was she very averse to anything. As a child she did all that average children do at every stage in life. At school she did not come first nor was she the last, but hovered somewhere in the middle. All her friends were just average friends who never got into trouble and never did anything very exciting.

They would watch TV together, play or study in a group and occasionally go to a movie. Shashikala never complained and never felt left out of the more exciting activities of all the other girls and boys her age.

We meet thousands of people in our lives and yet no two are the same. Each one is an individual and we usually remember them because there is always one trait or feature that sets them apart. While some are beautiful enough or ugly enough to make an impact, most leave an impression because of the shape of the nose, eyes or head, the manner of speaking, the tenor of their voice or the presence or absence of a distinct charisma. Shashikala, however, did not have any singular quality. Even if you had met her many times, you may not recognize her immediately. She was always part of the background, a part of the larger picture.

As a child at home; as a student in school; as a teenager or as a college student she was part of the crowd, a dot among many other dots. Her dreams too were not ambitious, not inspired by the legendry figures at home or abroad. She had no highs or lows. She did not veer back and forth from being ecstatically happy to being miserably depressed, as many young people tend to be. She had no great identity crisis and accepted herself for what she was. She did not plan her future or aspire to a successful career in any particular profession. She did not have romantic dreams of a knight in shining armour sweeping her off her feet.

In keeping with her personality and pattern in life, her parents arranged her marriage to a man who was also just about average. Akash was a balding, nondescript man with a clerical job in a big bank. He was not very keen on promotions or transfers because he had no interest in working harder or longer. He preferred to do his job with the ease and comfort of having done the same thing millions of times rather than get stressed out by joining the rat race. He was not a bad husband and did not demand very much except fairly good meals at the proper time and was happy to be left alone to watch the sports and news channels and read the papers.

Shashi was equally happy providing the meals and leaving him to his own devices in return for being left alone to do whatever she liked best which was reading some murder mysteries, especially those by Agatha Christie and *Mills and Boon* romances.

Their house was fairly clean but not scrupulously so, with a minimal effort at interior decoration. Shashi never bothered to dust the house unless she had guests. She coped with all the ups and downs of life—and there were not that many—with some measure of common sense. When her father died it made sense to bring her mother to live with them. When her mother was too ill it made sense to move her into a nursing home. There was no heartache or agonizing involved over what was right or wrong. It was more a question of common sense and convenience.

Two children were born without much fuss or bother and grew up as all children do with minor illnesses and coughs and colds. The parents found joy in the children's first steps and first words; taught them nursery rhymes and alphabets and took pride in their performances before their friends and family.

When both the children were quite grown up, Shashi, for the first time in her life, began to think of what she could do with herself. Even then, she did not think of it as a career of her own. It was more a question of being occupied and earning some money at the same time that would come in handy for the marriage of her daughter and their son's higher education. She did not even think of it the other way around—that she may need the money for her daughter's higher education and her son's marriage—conditioned as she was to the middle-class mentality.

At around the same time, there was news of the renovation of an old derelict building near the beach in Versova that had remained locked up for many years. The grand niece of the former owner came from abroad and transformed the old building into a guesthouse retaining much of the outer and inner décor. The intention was to make it a heritage hotel on a small scale, not very fancy but comfortable with an old-world charm and basic home-cooked food.

Shashi joined the staff to help with the housekeeping. Being of average intelligence, she mastered the art of making beds, changing linen, and tidying rooms without much difficulty. In fact, she was pleasantly surprised that she got paid for doing what she normally did at home only on a better and larger scale. She learnt the right way to turn down the sheet, where to tuck it in and how to fold it. She liked the work that did not need great training but a certain degree of conscientious attitude.

She also liked the way the building had been renovated. There was a large room in the front which had been turned into a foyer and there were two wings of four rooms each on either side of the lobby. The first three rooms on either side were bedrooms and the last room was the dining room and the business centre. In between the two wings, was a long corridor that ran the whole length, connecting the foyer in the front to the kitchen at the back. This corridor was Shashi's work space, her very own territory. Once the door was closed no one could even see it from the outside, as it all fitted into the woodwork so beautifully. This was her secret world, her domain and Shashi enjoyed the anonymity of working behind the scenes, unheard, unseen. She was in charge of this storehouse and had to ensure that it was always well-stocked to meet the requirements of the clients. She did her job meticulously and in the course of time the staff became accustomed to turn to her for all housekeeping problems.

She had an assistant, a rather mousey-looking girl who was as efficient as she was quiet. In fact, over time, Shashikala became quite fond of the girl and they worked very well together. She perhaps saw a little bit of herself in Minnie, but whatever it was, there was a fairly strong bond, an understanding and maybe even a certain amount of affection between the two.

After twelve years of the same routine Shashikala could do her job with practiced ease. Her nest egg was growing. Akash and Shashi were not big spenders and they had no desire to go in for a bigger TV or a fancy cooking range. Their holidays consisted of visiting their families in other cities and that too usually for a purpose such as a wedding, a housewarming ceremony, or a special anniversary or birthday. They were content to watch the travel channel on the television for visits to exotic destinations rather than spend money and energy touring around. At the age of fifty, Shashikala presumed she would have another ten years of service though some would call it drudgery. They were also happy that their twenty-year-old son and fifteen-year-old daughter were both cast in the same mould as their parents and had no inclination towards all the fads and pressures of their peer group.

Life for the little family was a smooth ride on well-oiled wheels of routine and there was a certain contentment in doing the same things every day. Shashi's walk to Churchgate station from their flat took all of fifteen minutes. She preferred the ladies' compartment but occasionally, if there was a lot of rush, she got into any compartment possible. As soon as she found a seat she would take out a *Mills and Boon* book, settle herself comfortably and lose herself in the world of dark, handsome, domineering men and bold, feisty women who fought with each other till they kissed and realized they were in love. Over the years she saw that the romantic stories deteriorated a bit and tended to be more like soft porn—a sign of the changing times of which she did not wholly approve. She liked it better when the hero and heroine kissed more than halfway through the story unlike now when they got into bed on the very first page or chapter. But she soon began to choose the book according to the author and tried to avoid the soft porn ones.

Once she was settled with her nose in a book, Shashi would not even look up till she neared Andheri, for she could identify the stations by their smells. She would get down at Andheri and take a rickshaw to her place of work and follow the same routine in reverse on the way back.

Friday, the 13th of November, however, turned out to be a very different day. It was far from being a routine day. There was a heavy load of work with Minnie on sick leave and she took more time to finish her work. Then, at the last minute there was an emergency booking and a room had to be immediately readied for a rich client.

She missed her usual train back home, could not get into the ladies' compartment but managed to enter a fairly crowded one next to that. There was no place to sit but rather surprisingly one young man stood up and offered her his seat and she did not refuse. It was not often that men gallantly gave up their seats these days. Within minutes she had her nose buried in her book and the rest of the world receded into the background. She was vaguely aware of shuffling feet and rustling of clothes, people getting off and on and a general thinning of the crowd.

At Bandra, four young men got into the train, talking loudly and laughing even more loudly. Shashi looked up briefly. All the four boys were dressed in cheap jeans and garish t-shirts. Three of them had unkempt hair and stubble or a beard. The fourth had a crew cut, thin sharp features and earrings in addition to a variety of rings and chains. With a sigh Shashi went back to her book with a silent prayer of gratitude that her son was not like them. She hoped that they would not be too disruptive because she was at an interesting part of the story. The hero and heroine were in the middle of a wordy duel—repartees and ripostes flying thick and fast with a lot of sarcasm and humour—and any moment the argument could end in a passionate embrace.

However, that was not to be. Much to her frustration the bawdy jokes and laughter of the boys spoilt all the charm of the story. She tried to ignore it all but the mutterings of disgust from the old man next to her made her look up again. The boys were now standing near two fairly well-dressed young girls seated on the right. One of them looked like an Anglo-Indian and wore a short skirt and top while the other was in a salwar and short kurti.

The boys made exaggerated lurching movements as the train gathered speed or slowed down, pretending to lose their balance and falling all over them. Jokes, comments and snatches of Hindi film songs seemed to provide them great amusement.

The girls tried to draw away and huddle closer together. The one wearing a mini skirt tried to cover her legs with her bag. They turned towards the window pretending to ignore the boys but Shashi could see the fear on their faces.

At the next station many more people got off. One of the boys sat down pushing himself against the girls. Shashi kept her book up, protectively, wanting to blot out what was happening in front of her. Suddenly, the elderly man on her left stood up and moved towards the boys shouting in anger. Just as suddenly the boy with the crew cut took a swipe at the old man and sent him reeling back. He fell with his back smashing against a seat and a couple of people helped him off the floor and made him sit up. The boy's ring had cut a thin red streak on his cheek that slowly welled up with blood and he was breathing in short gasps.

There were now only about fifteen commuters scattered around the compartment. One of them was a thin, bespectacled teenager who seemed highly agitated while his mother next to him held his arm restraining him from doing anything foolhardy. Some of the people in the compartment spoke to each other in undertones while others tried to look away as if they could not see or hear anything.

Shashi had lost all interest in her book now though she still held it open in her hand. She felt as helpless and ashamed as all the rest around her, afraid to get involved. The boy sitting next to the girls stretched out his arm behind them and let his fingers caress the back of the girl next to the window. Cornered and with a spurt of anger the girl turned around and slapped his hand. This made them laugh even more and the boy held the hand that slapped him. Meanwhile, another boy put his hand on the girl's knee, his dark hand a striking contrast against the fair skin.

The thin, bespectacled boy could bear it no longer. He broke free from his mother's grasp and lunged forward, his hand punching and hitting wildly. Two of the thugs now turned their attention on the teenager. They pummelled and kicked him while the mother looked on helplessly. She cried and implored but none of the passengers moved. There was a flash of steel and a sharp penknife ripped the teenager's shirt which was soon stained red by the cut underneath. Now no one dared to move or speak.

The wounded boy grew pale with fright and shock and his mother was almost on the verge of collapsing. She got up and staggered to his side, tearing a part of her sari to stem the flow of blood. Two of the four boys looked slightly chastened and wanted to move away but the other two shouted them down. A heated argument between the four ended in the crew cut leader yanking the boy sitting next to the girls. He punched him in the stomach and pushed him across to the other end. He sat down next to the girls himself and his thin dark fingers with flashy rings played with her hair.

Just at that moment the girl looked straight into Shashi's eyes. The pleading look and the direct eye contact hit Shashi like a body blow. The eyes were not that of a stranger. It was like looking into her daughter's eyes or Minnie's eyes. Shashi tried to look away but found it impossible to move her gaze from the girl's face. Although it perhaps lasted only a few seconds it seemed like a long time to Shashi. Something snapped within her and before she even realized it Shashi leapt to her feet. In the same movement, she snatched the big black umbrella from the hands of the man to her right (when had she noticed the umbrella and what was she going to do with it?) She quickly stretched out and put the curved hook-like end around the crew cut boy's neck and pulled hard with all her might. At the same time she let out a clarion call. 'Get up everyone. Attack them. Uttho! Uttho! Maaro!Maaro! Maaro!'

The crew cut boy was gagging as the hooked-end of the umbrella cut into his throat and he lost his balance. Momentarily, the thugs were taken by surprise. The small mousey woman was the last person they had expected to strike back. Galvanized by her call the people in the compartment all rose as one. Anything that they had in hand was turned into a weapon. Handbags, tiffin boxes and water bottles were swung by the handle, a briefcase landed squarely and heavily on the crew cut head, a few other satchels, shopping bags and umbrellas rained blows on the four hooligans.

Some passengers got bruised. One got a black eye and another had a cut lip. Dishevelled hair, shirts half pulled out of pants, broken or lost spectacles did not dim the feeling of unrestrained energy and courage. The boys cowered in the face of combined wrath. One of them was dazed having been hit on the head many times. Two sat on the floor nursing their wounds. By this time they were near Grant Road station and as the train slowed down one of the boys managed to jump out and escape.

Shashi's hair had become undone; her dupatta was on the floor and badly trampled upon. She had a bruise near her jaw and a small gash on her forearm. She was acknowledged the heroine of the day and many said if not for her initiative they would not have had the courage to move together. There was a general air of celebration and the helplessness was replaced by a sense of satisfaction and camaraderie.

Meanwhile, the thin bespectacled boy who had been hurt earlier had called the police and an ambulance on his cell phone. So by the time the train pulled into Churchgate the platform was teeming with police, journalists and a TV crew that had been in the vicinity. The police took down names and numbers and cameras kept flashing on and off.

Shashi was suddenly very tired and all she wanted to do was to get away from everything and everyone. But she was hemmed in by people on all sides, with questions flowing from every direction. Her legs felt like jelly. When she tried to walk away a strong light impaled her and as she stood frozen to the spot, a reporter pushed a microphone in front of her face and asked 'What does it feel like to be a hero? Have you always been a leader and a fighter?'

Shashi blinked through her spectacles that were slightly askew. The glare of the light blinded her and all she wanted was to go home. She swallowed a lump in her throat.

'No. I am not a leader or a fighter' she spluttered. 'I am just an average person,' she said, blinking away the tears that threatened to flow.

Stick Figures

VRINDA BALIGA

T arun's mother is not at the gate.

Tarun has put on his shoes and strapped the bag, containing his lunch-box and Spiderman toy, to his back. He is all set to leave, except for the tiny problem of his mother not being at the gate to collect him.

Tarun is standing on the narrow veranda of a squat single-storey house that belongs to Sara Joseph—Sara Aunty to the kids—who runs a day-care centre out of her living room. The house marks the end of the lane and is positioned perpendicular to the other houses, so that from where he stands, Tarun can see the entire lane till the point it meets the main road. His eyes scan the junction anxiously. He is usually among the first to leave. Behind him, there is a flurry of activity on the veranda as the other kids gather their things and put on their shoes.

Sara Aunty stands at the gate, summoning the kids one by one as their mothers arrive. Antara, Vikram, Amit, Meena…soon, everyone else has left. Sara Aunty latches the gate and turns around, the smile meant for the last parent still on her face. It vanishes, however, when she spots the solitary child on the veranda.

'Tarun? You're still here?'

Tarun shuffles his feet. Sara Aunty glances over her shoulder, expecting to see the familiar figure of Tarun's mother hurrying awkwardly down the lane in a sari, an attire she is not used to (as she has explained more than once to Sara Aunty in an apologetic tone), but has to wear because it is the mandated dress code for teachers at the school she has recently joined. The lane is empty.

Sara Aunty turns back to Tarun. 'Did she say she would be late today?'

He shakes his head.

Sara Aunty clicks her tongue in exasperation. 'Alright then, come on back inside.'

Tarun reluctantly takes off his shoes and follows her indoors, almost bumping into her as she suddenly stoops to pick up a stray crayon.

'You kids should learn to put things in their proper places,' she says. 'All this bending doesn't do much good for my back, you know.' She points him in the direction of a chair. 'Sit there and try not to get in my way.'

The furniture in the room is pushed to the walls during the day to make room for the day-care kids. That is the only concession Sara Aunty allows. She has made no attempt whatsoever to brighten the place up for the kids. There are no toys, except for the row of wobbly-headed wooden Chennapatna dolls in the show-case, but those are strictly off-limits to the kids.

Sara Aunty now walks around the room restoring order, all the while muttering to herself.

'You'd think people would call if they're going to be late! But, no! Take me for granted, that's what it is. After all I'm just an old woman with nothing better to do with my time...'

She straightens the chairs, drags the wicker rocking chair to its spot under the fan, and returns the glass vase to the side-table from its temporary refuge at the top of the television cabinet.

In the mornings, Sara Aunty is usually busy with her cooking and cleaning and leaves the kids largely to their own devices. They are allowed to bring a toy each from home and by now, they have made and ironed out among themselves, the complex set of rules that govern the sharing and barter of these toys. In the afternoons, however, she sits in her rocking chair in a corner of the room, with an eye on the clock, having started a mental countdown to the time when her home and she can be released from the grip of their presence. The hour hand of the wall-clock edges away from one o'clock, and it appears to the kids that the room begins to shrink. Her mounting impatience expands to fill it ('No, no, no, don't do that!', 'Stop that noise!', 'Sit down!') till finally, at 3.00 p.m., it virtually nudges them out onto the veranda.

Now, she casts a martyred look at the one obstacle that stands between her and her afternoon nap.

'Okay, what will you do till your mother comes?' she says, looking around. 'Something quiet, I hope. How about drawing?' She tears a couple of sheets from a sketch pad and puts them on the coffee table with a pencil and a box of crayons. Pulling up a plastic stool for him to sit on, she says, 'Don't make a mess now. Take the crayons out one at a time... And put them back once you're done. Is that understood?'

She settles into the rocking chair and switches on the television. Tarun hesitates, then picks up a sheet of paper. He draws with slow deliberation, the pencil exerting much more pressure on the paper than required. The shape of a boy appears—a circle for the face, lines for torso, arms and legs. Eyes, smile, spiky hair.

To his left, he draws his father. A square torso with buttons running down it. Trousered legs. A face with the brows drawn down in a dark 'V' over the eyes. Pa is always in a foul mood these days. Tarun has only a dim idea that it has something to do with a market that has crashed for some reason. Why can't Pa simply go to another market is something he hasn't figured out yet.

'Ma, what's eco-money?' he'd asked once when she was putting him to bed.

She had looked at him blankly for a moment, then understood. 'Economy,' she'd corrected. 'But you're right, it's something to do with money.' She had given him a long look and then patted his shoulder. 'These are not things for you to worry about, dear. Now, go to sleep.'

There are other words Pa spouts at the dinner table that Tarun instinctively knows better than to ask the meaning of.

To his right, he draws his mother. A wide smile, short hair coloured in with a black crayon. A big circle for the torso.

Ma's tummy isn't really big yet. But it will get 'round as a ball' soon. She had asked, 'So, dear, d'you want a baby brother or sister?'

A sister, he had decided after some thought. And she had laughed in delight.

Nowadays though, what with Pa's bad temper and her new job and Tarun's having to go to day-care, she doesn't laugh and joke like before. She is quiet and tired most of the time. This morning, she didn't speak a word to him when she walked him to Sara Aunty's house. Nor did she give him a hug when they reached. And when he looked back from the veranda, she was already walking away, instead of waiting at the gate with the usual wave and flying kiss.

At home too, at the dinner table, she has taken to sitting in tight-lipped silence. And the quieter she is, the angrier Pa seems to get.

'Don't sit there with that look on your face,' he shouts at

her. 'You didn't complain when things were going well, did you? Everything I do is for this family. You're the one who wants a house overrun with kids, don't you?'

Tarun looks at the picture. Ma, Pa, himself. That leaves only the baby, and the pencil now hovers uncertainly over the paper.

Pa says there will be no baby.

'This one will begin school next year,' he says, an angry finger pointing at Tarun. 'Do you know what the fees are like? It takes more to teach kids A-B-C and a couple of rhymes these days than it took me to complete my degree! How do you suppose we can afford one more?'

Sometimes, Ma is crying when she comes to tuck him in at night. She takes his hand and puts it on her stomach.

'There's a baby sister for you in there,' she says. 'Don't you ever forget that.'

'I can't feel her,' he says.

'Soon,' she says. 'Soon, she will start kicking. Then, everything will be alright. Just a little more time...'

Making his mind up, Tarun draws a tiny girl in Ma's tummy. He folds the paper and puts it in his pocket. He puts the crayons back in their box. Sara Aunty is snoring on the rocking chair. The television drones on with the news. And Ma still hasn't arrived.

It is dark when the doorbell finally rings. Tarun's father is at the door. This is the first time he has come to collect Tarun from Sara Aunty's house.

Sara Aunty speaks to him sharply, 'This is simply not acceptable, Mr Parab...'

In response, Pa merely nods, offering neither explanation, nor apology. He lifts Tarun up and carries him all the way to the motorcycle, something he hasn't done in ages.

By the time they reach home, Ma has gone to bed. 'She's very tired,' Pa says. 'Don't disturb her.'

He says nothing, however, when Tarun runs to her bedroom. Ma is not asleep. She is lying very still on the bed and staring at the ceiling. He climbs onto the bed and slips under the covers. She doesn't seem to notice. After a few seconds, he rests his hand lightly on her stomach. She pushes it away and turns to the wall.

•◆

A Cup of Tea

PARITOSH UTTAM

The first thought that struck Abhijit Gupta as soon as he awoke was that it was Wednesday. It put him in a vile mood straight away. The middle of the week—it seemed to him that he had been going to work for days on end but the weekend was nowhere in sight. Not that he loved his home, but he preferred his wife's company to his boss's. Again, not because he loved his wife dearly, but because he didn't have to hear his boss's scornful hollering, and could instead scream at his wife and his son. At home, he was the boss. Abhijit liked the idea and smiled to himself. The smile turned into a frown when he heard a little snore. He turned to his right and ran his eyes over his supine wife and watched soft snores escape her half-open mouth. He was filled with disgust. He shook her roughly.

'Wake up! Do you want to sleep all day? Get me a cup of tea.' Mrs Gupta woke with a start, sat up for a few moments to recover her bearings, and then slipped silently into the bathroom.

Abhijit could not get rid of the disgust. How could a young, attractive woman turn into this slovenly creature that was his wife, in a matter of a few years? He felt he had been tricked. He distinctly remembered the svelte woman he had married five years ago. She bore no resemblance to the plump woman who snored in bed beside him, and was now brushing and spitting in the bathroom with appalling noisiness. Someone had replaced his wife when he was not looking.

Abhijit's mood didn't lighten on his way to the office. The jostling for a foothold in the 9.32 CST Fast and the fight to retain his standing space were bound to put any man out of humour. But the resentment that surged within him was directed at his wife, not his fellow commuters. Why didn't she take the least bit of care regarding her appearance? Why did she fill him with such loathing? She looked after his needs well and he knew that he would be very uncomfortable without her. But he despised her. He couldn't get around that fact.

Her passivity infuriated him. Why didn't she have more life in her? Why wasn't she more demonstrative? His impatience with her lethargy caused friction and forced out a few stifled sobs from her. He would then feel guilty and irritated and try to make it up in bed. But it was a vicious cycle. The sight of all that flab around her waist and thighs repulsed him; he wished he hadn't tried. He behaved like a brute. He pinched, squeezed and bit her. He wanted her to cry out and protest. She didn't. She bore it heroically. This maddened him and he worked himself up into a bestial fury.

Abhijit finally reached his office. When he saw Anju, the boss's personal secretary, his spirits rose, but the joy was short-lived. His boss sent for him and railed at him for ten minutes for what Abhijit considered a minor error. It was a standing joke in the office that whenever the boss suffered from constipation, he made someone else suffer too.

When the boss was through with him, Abhijit was left to his own thoughts. He was damned if he was going to work that day, after the humiliation he had been put through, and that too within Anju's hearing. Why wasn't his wife like Anju? He could then have gladly taken her to movies and restaurants, which she complained he never did. What if he had been married to Anju? Somehow he couldn't imagine her bringing him a cup of tea first thing in the morning after being jolted awake. He wanted a woman who was vivacious as well as obsequious. Abhijit was aware of the inherent contradictions in his fantasies, but he shrugged them off. The very least he could do, in his life that was otherwise full of compromises, was to not compromise in his dreams.

Of all the girls in college, why had he chosen her and asked her to marry him? For the life of him, he could not remember now any reason that compelling. Perhaps she was the only one who had encouraged him, and thus soothed his ego. But was that reason enough to marry so early, in the face of opposition from both sets of parents? He had also foolishly told her that she did not have to work after marriage because he was duty-bound to be the breadwinner. However, as a proof of his broadmindedness, he gallantly left her the option of working if she wanted to. Of course she declined, knowing very well that she was unemployable. She saw him as her gateway to a life of freedom and security. Within a year of marriage, she presented him with a son—and that was it, she was done.

Finally, the clock struck five; Abhijit had got through with the day. He sprang from his chair with a sigh of relief, collected his bag and hurried out. Yet, he walked with leaden feet. He was going back home to his wife who nagged him, or gave him reproachful looks for confining their family to a one-bedroom apartment in Kandivili, while her classmates had moved to bigger houses in better localities. Did she expect him, on the basis of his single salary, to not only provide for all of them, but also save enough to afford a bigger house in Mumbai? When he returned home in the evening, exhausted and battered after the day's work and the crowded train journey back with his nose buried in someone's sweaty armpit, he did not have the strength in him to think about or prepare for a better job. Any constructive thought or work was not possible in the presence of his wife, or his pesky four-year old, who began bawling at the lightest touch.

His wife would open the door, take his bag and he would ask her for a cup of tea. The same sequence of events would unfold the next day. And the next. Week after week. He screamed. His life would be over, shuttling to and fro, from home to office. He was serving a sentence of life imprisonment in an open jail. Something would have to change. Or whatever was left of him would be blown to smithereens from within.

As soon as his wife opened the door, he would spring it on her. He would tell her he wanted a divorce. He wanted to see the shock register on her face and see how long it would take for the message to percolate through her thick skull. She could go back to her parents and take the boy with her. Even if she didn't agree to a divorce, he would go away. He would try his hand at something else. He didn't know what, but he would do something—once free and unbound, the possibilities were limitless. All that would come later. Right now, he didn't care. He only wanted to break free from his hell.

Abhijit felt happy. He was getting out at last. His heart beat fast as he approached his house, but was relieved to note that he didn't suffer any pang of remorse. There would be enough time for remorse later, if it ever came to that. He could hear his heart pounding as he stood before the door. He took a deep breath and jabbed at the doorbell.

Susila Gupta was in too much of a hurry that morning to

be angry with her husband for shaking her awake so rudely. She bustled from the bathroom to the kitchen to the dining table in her nightgown with an economy and fluency that came solely with years of experience. She knew his demands weren't that urgent, that there were local trains every five minutes, but she didn't want to give him an excuse to shout at her again. She was inured to his ranting by now. Nevertheless, she found solace in grumbling to herself. After Abhijit left for office, she packed her son off to kindergarten in the school bus, and she had the house to herself. She could set her own pace now. She grumbled while cleaning the dishes and operating the washing machine. Today, the complaints to her own ears echoed louder than usual.

'Couldn't he let me sleep for a few more minutes? What difference would it have made to him? He read the newspaper for ten minutes after breakfast and he did it on purpose, just to show me that he wasn't really in a hurry. Why is he like that? I work so hard to keep him happy.'

Usually, the grumbling ceased with her household chores, after which she relaxed in her bath. But today, it showed no signs of ceasing.

'Is it only my duty to look after our son? Feed him, buy or mend his clothes, bathe him, put him in the school bus with his tiffin box, pick him up, put him to bed, everything? Will someone tell me what a father's duties are? He behaves as if he's got nothing to do with him, as if it were all my doing.'

Susila Gupta (nee Agarwal) was the third of four daughters in a typically lower middle-class family and hadn't enjoyed any special privileges in her childhood. Her most thrilling moment in life was in her final year in college when Abhijit had proposed to her. It would be her first proposal, as well as the last, and she grabbed it with both hands, not letting go even in the face of staunch opposition from her parents. She pinned all her hopes on marriage and looked forward to it because she believed it offered her the promise of a better life. She cried perfunctorily at the wedding, and was actually more lost in contemplation of her new life than anything else. She had been glad to get away.

All her expectations were quelled within the first few months when she became pregnant, and within a year she had cried herself into accepting the inevitable. Today, after five years, she subjected herself to severe self-questioning.

'Why propose to me, if he does not love me? Did anyone force him to? He told me himself that I need not work, and now he feels I am a burden on him. That's why he cannot take me out to movies or dinner, he says, because a single salary does not go far these days. And then why the shock when I became pregnant? He doesn't know what he wants.'

Susila was convinced she had arrived at the correct conclusion: her husband was confused.

'Doesn't everybody age? If I carry his child in me for nine months, won't I put on weight? Am I Kareena Kapoor to spend half my life in the gym to look thin? What about him? He's short, has a paunch, and has started losing hair. All he does is loll around the house.'

She noticed contusions near her left breast. Her eyes welled up with tears. 'He's a brute, an animal. His mouth reeks of onion. He doesn't even bother to brush before…' She shut her eyes tightly, feeling miserable. And felt alien thoughts visiting her mind. 'What does he really want or expect of me?'

'It's got to change. I can't take it anymore. I'll ask him to treat me better. Or I won't budge inside the house. I'm not a waiter, whose job it is to serve him cups of tea and carry out orders. His duties don't end at merely providing for us. As soon as he comes home today and asks for his tea, I will tell him he cannot take me for granted anymore. There's no point in putting it off and hoping he'll turn a new leaf one fine morning.'

Susila was surprised at her own boldness, but was also convinced that it was high time. She then settled down to watch the afternoon serial on TV, but couldn't concentrate and almost forgot that she had to go down to pick her son up, until the impatient blaring horn of the school bus reminded her. As the hands of the clock crept towards six, she was aware of a quickness in her pulse. The doorbell jangled. She froze, stricken by panic. She collected herself and walked slowly towards the door. Her fingers trembled as she took off the latch and pulled the door open.

Abhijit stared at her. Susila met his stare with her own unwavering gaze. Both stood still. Abhijit swallowed twice. Then he took a step inside, held out his hand, and heard himself forming the words, 'Get me a cup of tea.'

Susila took the bag from him, put it on the table and walked into the kitchen to put the kettle on boil.

•◆

The Enlightened One

HASMITA CHANDER

The ascetic sat under the banyan tree, meditating. His hair was long, like his beard. His arms stretched forward so that his wrists rested on his bony knees. His legs were crossed, his ankles oblivious to the roughness of the earth under him. The cacophony of the forest bounced off his concentration.

He had lived here for four years. He was known as Shanti Baba, the peaceful hermit. He listened to people's troubles but spoke little. When Baba looked at them, people were filled with the inner strength to handle their troubles.

The people who lived around the forest brought him food. They built him a thatched hut and provided the essentials.

The hermit's food varied with the people bringing it, but for the last seven months, he had eaten a daily lunch of warm chapattis, a vegetable side dish and a bowl of dal. He looked forward to this meal and the person who brought it: Raghunath Bhosle.

Finished with his meditation, the hermit rubbed his hands together, placed them over his face and slowly opened his eyes. It was past midday.

He went for his customary walk to stretch his limbs. When he reached his hut, Raghunath Bhosle was waiting for him.

The reedy old man folded his hands in a namaste when he saw the hermit, who returned the gesture. 'Have you been waiting long, Bhosleji?'

'Not at all, I just arrived, Baba. Will you eat your meal while it is hot?'

Every day Bhosle made this offer, and the hermit answered in a similar manner.

'No, Bhosleji, let us talk a little. How was work today?'

The old man squatted, rested his back against the wall, and sighed.

'All as usual, Baba, what can change? Nothing. The young men who work beside me, they talk and joke around all the time. They are always finding ways to shirk their work. When the supervisor is not around they play card games or chat and smoke. Who will do the work allotted to them?'

'I hope you don't try to do their work for them?'

'The supervisor is an unreasonable man. He always says, "Why is the work going so slow?" and glares at me, as if only I can be the reason, because of my weak, old body. The young ones never speak up. But I just do my job and keep quiet.'

'And how is your dog, Tipu? Is he eating better now?'

'You remembered, Baba.' A smile relaxed his face. 'Yes, he had his chapattis and milk today. His stomach has recovered, I think.'

Then Bhosle said, 'Baba, I'm sorry, I always ramble on and on. You must be hungry! Will you eat?'

As usual, the hermit said, 'Won't you join me?'

And the old man replied, 'No, Baba, I'll eat at home. Tipu will be waiting for me.'

The hermit ate the chapattis with relish, using them to scoop up the warm dal. At intervals, he bit into the raw onion accompanying the chapattis to spice up the taste.

In his other life, Uday Ghatge's job had been to convince companies to buy financial software packages. He received a good salary and earned a commission on each sale he brought about.

Uday was a smooth talker. He was not intimidated by technology and made it his business to know why his products were better than the competition. He also didn't hesitate to lie his way out of a tight spot.

He got every job he was interviewed for, and lost no time jumping from one company to the next, each time with a swell in pay.

In Mumbai's rat race, Uday was in the lead. He wasn't the biggest or the fastest, but he knew the shortcuts to win the race. He got his cleverness from his mother, his anchor, Heera Ghatge.

After giving birth to two girls, Mrs Ghatge had been blessed with the male child she had prayed for: Uday. Naturally, she had big dreams for him.

Mrs Ghatge raised her son differently from her daughters. The girls were taught to cook, clean, and sew. They would be married off to wealthy men lured by the girls' beauty and tidy dowries, already put by, thanks to the insurance received on Mr Ghatge's demise. Mr Ghatge was sixteen years senior to his wife and died of a massive heart attack at the age of fifty-four. Mrs Ghatge recovered quickly from her husband's death. She had what she had married him for—a comfortable lifestyle, enough money to last her till the end, and a son—a handsome, adorable boy.

Uday was not close to his sisters, being much younger and treated more specially than them. He enjoyed making his mother laugh with his antics and naughty pranks; her laughter encouraged him to go a step farther each time. What he couldn't bear were her silences. When he displeased her, she shut him out and refused to acknowledge his presence.

When he was nine, Uday stole a slab of chocolate from a general store. The shopkeeper caught him red-handed and complained to his mother. Mrs Ghatge slapped Uday and made him apologise to the shopkeeper.

Uday got her unbearable silence all the way home.

He sobbed. 'Sorry, Ma? Please, Ma, sorry! I'll not steal again, Ma!'

She didn't look at him.

After two hours of her torturing silence, Uday brought a matchbox.

'Ma, I'll burn my hand!'

Mrs Ghatge watched television.

Uday lit a match. Fire licked one finger. He screamed and dropped the match. Then his mother looked at him.

She got up and struck him with the back of her hand. He fell down, his head stinging worse than his finger. She returned to the television. Uday applied some ice on his finger and went to his room, where he brooded the rest of the day.

His mother spoke to him to the next day. He discovered that she was so furious because, thanks to Uday, that worm of a shopkeeper could point a finger at her. He learnt two things from this episode.

One: it's not wrong to steal, but he mustn't get caught doing it. Two: instead of fighting his mother's silences, he should ignore them—as she ignored him.

Seeing that her silence no longer affected him, Heera Ghatge resorted to shouting at him instead. This, Uday could handle. He sweet-talked his way out of trouble, and usually made sure she never discovered he had been up to any.

When Uday's heart leapt and hammered at the sight of Aparna, he kept his feelings secret from his mother.

Aparna was a science student in the college opposite his place of work. At four in the evening, Uday would peek through the vertical blinds by his desk; she would be standing near the college gate, waiting for her car. No local trains for her, apparently. She was slim, fair, and had pouty pink lips. She wore rimless glasses, trendy clothes, and left her hair open like a shawl about her shoulders. He saw Aparna scolding her driver almost every day—the fellow was often late, to Uday's delight. He could watch her that much longer.

The hermit's life in the forest was comfortable due to his devotees' kindness, but mainly, he was grateful for Bhosle.

After making his usual enquiries one day, the hermit said, 'Bhosleji, I would like to come and thank your wife for these delicious meals you bring me every day.'

Bhosle shook his head. 'No need for thanks, Baba. You're welcome to share my simple meal.'

Bhosle fingered his knuckles. 'If my wife had done the cooking, the chapattis would melt in your mouth, Baba—there was magic in her hands... She left this world eight years ago. Asthma.'

The hermit was surprised. Bhosle's clothes were in good repair. The food was good. And the old man seemed peaceful, too. 'I'm sorry to hear this, Bhosleji. It must be hard.'

The old man was silent awhile. 'I miss her presence in the house... but I have Tipu. He was already family when Saritha died, and he has been with me through difficult times. That dog is special, Baba. We understand each other even though we speak different languages.'

His face cracked up in a grin. 'It's true!'

Earlier, Uday Ghatge wouldn't have given a minute to a man like Bhosle. He had spent time hobnobbing with the influential people in his company, learning each man's weakness. When the time was right, Uday tapped that weak point and got his way with the man. The strategy always worked. In Mumbai, life was tough, a dog-eat-dog world, a world in which Uday thrived.

He stood to gain from Bhosle's acquaintance too. The man did provide the daily meal. But he had got by before Bhosle began to visit him, and he would get by now if the old man stopped coming.

Uday found himself thinking of his father, who had died when he was six. Uday had stopped speaking for several days then. His mother finally managed to make him cry after four days, releasing the pain inside him. He clung to her more than ever after that. Now he tried to remember his father, and couldn't. A memory surfaced, of the photograph framed in his house, but the face was a blur. What sprung up instead was Bhosle's familiar face.

Uday wondered how old Bhosle was. Sixty? Seventy? His face and body were so weathered, it was hard to tell.

One day, Bhosle said, 'Baba, can I ask you something? I hope you'll not find me inquisitive.'

The hermit had just finished lunch. 'Yes, ask me, what is it?'
'Who are you, Baba? From where have you come? Why are you here? I wonder about it often but didn't ask you.'

The hermit's nostrils flared in annoyance. Was the police making enquiries for a missing Uday Ghatge?

'What is it to you, Bhosleji? Did someone from the town send you to ask me this?'

Bhosle seemed not to have heard. He continued, 'You're an educated man, maybe with big achievements in a city. Yet, you're living as a hermit. You're young, too. So, what brought you here? Don't answer if you don't want to, Baba. I just thought talking might lighten your burden. I do not have a loose tongue.'

Uday took a deep breath and closed his eyes as he did while meditating. After a few more deep breaths, he was able to calm down.

'My mother's death.' There, he had said it.

'I could not think of a life without her,' he continued. 'My father died when I was little. My wife left me. All I had was Ma.'

Suddenly Uday wanted to talk. Thoughts of his mother flooded him.

'I have two sisters, but she loved me the most… She bought me anything I asked for, got me educated in a big school, the best college. To my chapattis and rice, she added dollops of ghee—my sisters got little or nothing. More than these little things, she believed in me. She said I'd grow up to be somebody one day. She didn't hope—she knew!'

Bhosle smiled. 'Yes, parents think their children are incarnations of God.'

'Whatever I am is because of her. I had a successful career in Mumbai. Within five years I went from being a trainee to a regional manager. If I had continued through these years, who knows where I would be now…'

Bhosle noticed the wistfulness on the hermit's face. 'Will you not return to your career, Baba? It seems a waste to leave behind all that success—'

'No!' he said at once. 'I'm at peace here. I have a different life now. I'm closer to God.'

Uday glanced at the deer grazing outside. He exhaled slowly. 'You know, Bhosleji, my mother was a devout woman. She would beg, threaten, and bribe the gods to do her bidding. Mostly for my sake!

'She once visited Amarnath through the worst snow and ice to beg Lord Shiva for a son. I was born within a year. After that she went there every year. She bore the cold, the five-day journey and the danger of terrorists there in Kashmir. Nothing stopped her. She hoped she would die there, too…'

The hermit's voice suddenly dropped to a whisper. Bhosle leaned forward to hear him. 'But that's not where she died. She didn't get… a holy ticket.'

Composure deserted Shanti Baba as his face crumpled. 'She died in a road accident! She was lying on the roadside when I reached her, already dead. There was so much blood and her face…' He closed his ears with his hands, his head bowed down, as if a bomb had exploded near him.

Bhosle looked down at his hands, twisting them gently. After a few moments, the hermit continued.

'I set fire to her pyre later, but I never stopped standing there on the roadside… staring at her. After the funeral, I didn't know what to do. I couldn't think. I sat on my motorbike and rode, not knowing where to. I got out of the city and kept going till my petrol ran out. I pushed the bike into a ditch and began to run. I ran and ran, until I saw this forest. It was shady and cool, its silence welcoming. I entered it to rest, to let it enfold me, take me into its womb. I've been here since then.'

Both men were silent for several minutes.

Then Bhosle said, 'Such a past! Yet, you became the peaceful hermit. Shanti Baba. It's a big thing that you've achieved peace in spite of it all.'

After Bhosle left, his words echoed in the hermit's ears.

'You've achieved peace in spite of it all.'

'Such a past!'

'Shanti Baba.'

Had he achieved peace? His mind flung pictures of Aparna at him. Aparna, whom he had wooed and married. The secret set-up by which they made it seem an arranged match; in which they met like strangers before their parents, and agreed with enough reluctance to seem genuine. His mother would never have agreed to a love match, and Aparna brought a good dowry as well.

But then, he had come home most days to Aparna's complaints about Ma.

One day she said, 'Why can't she leave us alone! From the time we got married you've hardly spent any time with just me. It's always Ma, Ma, Ma…'

He had snapped, 'You've come to our house. If you don't like it, leave!'

Aparna cried herself to sleep. He apologised the next day.

Three years into the marriage, things were the same. One night, in their bedroom, Aparna burst out: 'I wake up early, make breakfast and lunch, go to work travelling an hour each way by local train. It's trauma for me, getting pushed and shoved and learning to do it back to survive the journey! I come home ready to collapse and your mother doesn't even make me a cup of tea. What does she do all day? Even dinner I have to make. In this tiny kitchen!'

Before he could reply, she said, 'Okay, I won't ask, and I don't care what she does if she'd let me live my life in peace. But no! She won't let me visit my friends or family, and today when my colleague came home your mother insulted her way of dressing! When you come home, you go straight to her. If I join you, I'm included in the conversation; otherwise, I'm forgotten! I want to talk to you without her around. I'm forced to talk with her listening in and spouting unwanted advice, or must wait until we come to bed, where you fall asleep as I talk. I'm sick of this! I feel like a maid in this house, that's all!'

He had had enough of the frequent squabbles by then. 'Fine. So what do you want? You want to leave?'

Aparna had looked like a witch then, her hair in a mess, her eyes wide and edged with leaked surma. 'That's always the solution, isn't it? You won't change the situation, work things out. If I don't like it, I must decide whether to stay or leave!'

He shrugged.

'Then I've decided. I'll leave in the morning.'

And she left. Although he tried a few times to convince her to return, he didn't succeed. Six months later, Ma died.

He had almost gone to Aparna that day at the funeral. But he couldn't bear to hear a word against Ma. Or to hear that after choosing Ma over her, it was too late now to go back to Aparna.

He opened his eyes and focused on his surroundings. The banyan tree's aerial roots rippled in the breeze. A few rabbits nibbled at the vegetation a few feet away. Sunlight filtered through the tapestry of the forest canopy, winking and shimmering between the leaves.

The wrinkles on his forehead slowly relaxed and he returned to the harmony of the sylvan world.

A few days later, the hermit was disturbed shortly after he began his meditation. He heard sniffling and opened his eyes.

Bhosle was sitting before him, tears running down his face. The hermit held the old man's shoulders. 'What happened, Bhosleji?'

'Tipu…' Bhosle moaned. 'He's gone, Baba. First my son left me, then Saritha, and now my Tipu! Please, will you come and say a few words for him?'

Uday made his way to Bhosle's house. As they walked, Bhosle kept up a monologue about the dog. Tipu had had kidney trouble for a while but medicines had kept the problem under control. The previous evening he got a fever, which escalated over the night. By morning the dog gave up the fight to stay alive.

After walking about twenty minutes, Bhosle stepped off the rough path. The ground toasted Uday's feet through the worn soles of his slippers. The dry, red mud lifted like smoke with each step. His eyes burned in the harsh sunlight. A few thorny trees and patches of gold grass were the only vegetation around.

Two rows of barbed wire wound around wooden poles stuck in the ground served as a fence. There was no gate. The men walked into the house, which was cool despite the heat outside. It was not more luxurious than his thatched hut—a single-room dwelling, but made of brick and cement.

A stove and a few utensils stood in one corner. Containers of various sizes—some aluminium, some glass—held lentils, flour, rice, and spices. Near a sack, Uday saw a clean stainless steel bowl with water. It must have been the dog's.

A calendar with a picture of Lord Ganesha hung from a nail on the wall. Across the far end of the room stretched a coir rope over which a few clothes were draped. Uday drank the water Bhosle offered him and they stepped out in silence.

A straggly assortment of plants grew around the hut. Marigolds poked their bright orange heads out here and there but did little to beautify the scene. The curry leaf tree was the only strong one, covered in dark green leaves. The dog lay under this tree. It was a common brown mongrel, made a little ugly by a permanently-bared upper lip and an odd-length, cut-off tail, but it looked well fed and clean.

Uday watched Bhosle dig the grave. Being a hermit, he was not expected to help and he could not bring himself to. He watched mutely as the old man dug the shovel into the earth, his skin moving over his ribs and spine with each effort.

When it was done, Uday recited a prayer:

Om, Asato Maa Sadgamaya, Tamaso Maa Jyotirgamaya, Mrityormaa'mritam Gamaya.

Oh lord, lead me from untruth to truth, from darkness to light, from death to immortality.

With his hands cupped in the air above the dog, he said, 'God bless you for your companionship to a good man. Rest in peace.'

The men stood with their eyes closed, hands folded in prayer, Bhosle thinking of his family, Uday thinking of his own. Bhosle lowered the dog into the grave and covered it with earth.

The hermit returned from Bhosle's hut and, after a bath, sat under the banyan tree to meditate. He could not concentrate. His mind was still in the farmer's hut.

What struck him was the ordinariness of Bhosle's life. He lived alone in a spare home, surrounded by the dry, heat-absorbent land. He had only a mongrel to love. Now he had lost even the dog.

He saw again the old man's skin sliding over his bones as he dug the grave. Bhosle must have laboured in the fields all his life. What kept him going? What was his dream? Did he even have one? What gave him satisfaction?

Uday had dreamt of running his own business, owning swanky cars, and covering his mother and wife in jewellery. His wife… Did Aparna still think of him? Did she wonder where he was or had she stopped caring the day she had left his house?

Around noon, the hermit realised Bhosle would not come that day. No devotees had visited him the previous day either. He would have to find some food for himself.

Under the jamun tree on his walk route he found a handful of its succulent violet berries. He plucked a half-ripe fruit from a mango tree and headed back.

He need not have bothered. Bhosle was waiting in his hut, with hot lunch.

'Bhosleji!' Uday blurted. 'How come you're…? I thought you would need time to get over your loss. I know your dog meant much to you.'

The old man blinked rapidly, as if to stopper his tears.

His voice was feeble. 'I wanted to beg you to bury me, too,

Baba. I would lie next to Tipu and sleep forever, holding him. Inside the warm earth, dark and comforting, I would have gladly breathed my last.'

He stared at the banyan tree outside for several minutes. The tree's leaves rustled as if they, too, were discussing death and loss.

Uday brought him water. After sipping it, Bhosle looked at the hermit, his old irises ringed with grey. 'It is natural, I suppose, to feel such weakness, this panic, in the face of death. But… I have so many blessings, Baba. My dear daughters… I'm their only parent, their link to each other.'

Bhosle sighed. 'My stupid son is bound to return home some day. What if he arrived the day I buried myself? I have not yet repaid my debt to the landlord, Baba. If I died, he would pester my daughters.'

'I have my land, my work. I'm healthy enough to take care of myself. In this area I have friends whom I've known most of my life. I have your friendship, if I may say so, Baba.'

'Of course, of course,' Uday mumbled.

'My parents went through difficult times to bring me up. They are no more, but if they read my thoughts today from the other world, they would be ashamed of me.'

Uday looked at Bhosle squatting against the wall. Even inside the tiny hut, he was small. A small, impotent man.

Uday pondered on Bhosle's reaction to death and his own to his mother's death.

When the news hit him he had felt charcoal clouds seal the sky. The darkness blinded him. If he took another step he felt he would fall, fall deep into the chasm surrounding him. He was balanced on a sliver of land protruding from the earth.

Then, a piercing beam shot out of the clouds and focused on his mother's body. Her forehead was flattened into her skull, her brains splattered like a halo. Blood covered her, except for the contrasting green sari-shroud.

This was not his mother. No, no, no. This was only a smashed shell that had held Ma. Where was she?

Her soul would be whole, untouched. He had to find her soul, get away from this impermanent mess of a body.

Ma, I'm coming!

He went after her, not knowing where she had flown. He would find her. He would lie in her lap and bury his face in her belly and never let her go. He had not found her soul. Instead, in time, he had started searching for his own. He felt like a newborn: helpless, ignorant, without his mother. He wanted enlightenment on how the world worked, and where he fit in, and what he had to do.

Yet, he had been sitting here every day, closing his senses to the world around him, shutting out thought and emotion—aiming at nothingness. His efforts were rewarded. He had become an expert at attaining zero.

He lost himself in meditation, suspended in a void where nothing mattered.

He blocked out the memories of pleasure in his life: biting into a chunky candy bar, the cool air from an air conditioner on his sweaty skin, the smell of fish frying, staring at the Mumbai skyline at night from his twenty-eighth-floor apartment, and most of all, Aparna.

Her fingers kneading his aching back, the bell-like sound of her laughter, the texture of her lips in his mouth.

She would have probably been kind to him if he had gone to her that day. She wouldn't say anything against Ma, not then.

But he had felt hunted, as if the universe had conspired to punish him with Ma's death for choosing her over his wife. And so he had run away from the only person who could possibly have helped him.

Would she have married again? He had never let this thought surface, but today he let it come. Yes, she may have.

Uday opened his eyes. It was barely an hour since he had sat down to meditate, but he could not sit still any more. He got up and began to pace.

Would he ever get enlightenment? Was he willing to die waiting for it?

And what if it came to him, the great answer to life's questions?

He looked around. He would still be here in this forest, waiting for Bhosle's chapattis.

The static state of his existence hit him like a punch to the solar plexus. He saw himself sitting here for four years, doing nothing.

'Oh, God!' he cried and fell to his knees.

Tears oozed out of his tightly shut eyes. After all the dry-eyed years, he wept. He sobbed loud and long for his mother, for himself, and for his wife. He agonised over what he had done. When life walloped him with his mother's death, he had run away like a child from the bogeyman. His body shuddered with the force of the suppressed pain finding a release at last.

'But I haven't escaped, Lord! Ma is still dead. I've only made things worse for myself. I have no face to show anyone!'

Uday couldn't bear to be alone with his tormenting thoughts. He ran to Bhosle.

The old man was returning home after the day's work. When he saw the hermit running towards him, he dropped his tools and hurried to meet him. The hermit's eyes were red and his face was tear-streaked.

Uday clasped the old man and struggled to calm down. Bhosle's body was so delicate, Uday loosened his hold on him.

'Drink some water. Here,' Bhosle said.

Uday gulped the water and sat down on the floor of Bhosle's house.

'What is it, Baba? What has upset you?'

'I'm no Baba!' he shouted. 'I'm Uday Ghatge, didn't I tell you? I'm nothing but a fool! I'm a coward who ran away from his responsibilities and his life. That's the enlightenment I have received. The answer, the reward, to my penance!'

Bhosle said nothing. The old man's calmness enraged Uday.

'You knew it all along, didn't you! You were just being polite and letting me pretend all this time! You were indulging me!'

Bhosle pushed a refilled glass towards Uday, who looked ready to kick it away. But he picked it up and sipped. Then he went out and splashed water on his face, and ran wet fingers through his hair.

He came in, wiping his face. 'I'm sorry, I'm not myself. Or maybe this is who I am. I don't know! Help me, Bhosleji!' Tears began to leak out of his eyes again.

'I am an uneducated villager, son,' Bhosle said. 'I don't know what to advise you. You're intelligent and can think for yourself. I will help you any way I can.'

'What do I do, Bhosleji? Tell me what to do now!'

'What do you want to do?'

'I...I just want to just stay here, keep living one day at a time the way I've been doing. There is such peace here...'

Uday clutched his hair. 'But maybe I should go back to the city. That's what I should do. But I'm afraid to go back there...it's too hard, Bhosleji! Impossible!'

'Son,' Bhosle said, 'It would be even harder for you to live here after you've realised that.'

Shaved and wearing the clothes he had arrived in, Uday headed for the edge of the forest. The trousers stayed up only by his belt. He felt as if he were wearing somebody else's clothes. In a way, he was.

He had said goodbye to Bhosle, who would be one more companion short. But Raghunath Bhosle was not a lonely man.

Uday stepped out of the shade of the forest and into the sunlight on the road to the city.

◆

Dialects of Silence

VRINDA BALIGA

Dad often spoke of the first time he met Ma. Ma never did.

'We were to meet her family at the home of a common acquaintance,' Dad would begin. 'My new black shoes were way too tight, but your Ajji had insisted I wear them. You know how useless it is to protest once Ajji makes up her mind.' There would be sympathetic laughter here; my brother Amit and I often had run-ins of our own with our iron-willed grandmother. 'Ajji was ringing the doorbell and I was struggling to get those blasted shoes off when I saw them. The sequined sandals, half-hidden amidst the other footwear outside the door. I knew, in that instant, that they were hers...'

My teenage mind could well imagine Dad, a nervous young man, on his way to meet the woman he would probably spend the rest of his life with. What does he know about her beyond a couple of sepia photographs he's probably been shown? Even with this meeting, can he hope to glimpse her true personality from behind all the layers of propriety?

And then, he sees the pair of sequined sandals, and somehow

he is sure they are hers. Suddenly, unexpectedly, he feels he knows something about this person he is about to meet—a meagre, yet personal, detail—that the others don't, not even Ajji, who doubtless has the entire lowdown on the girl's family.

Though 'First Date', as we teasingly called it, was a personal favourite with Dad, it was by no means our only peek into our parents' lives. Dad had a talent for plucking an incident, a moment from the past, garnishing it with the minutest of details and presenting it to us, as fresh as if it had just happened. Amit and I had heard these stories many times over, but that never deterred Dad from giving them yet another airing. And truth be told, we loved them too, almost as much as we loved to corner him if we found inconsistencies from one telling to the next.

There was only one other person who could know how true Dad's stories really were. But Ma never corrected Dad. She never interrupted a story like we did, never said he was over-romanticizing something, or claimed that something had happened this way and not that. She was content with the way Dad was faithfully aging their joint memories over the years like good wine.

Thinking back now, it seems eerily like they knew, even back then, the roles they would play in later life.

I often wondered how you felt during that first meeting. Why didn't you have your own romantic version of it? Why didn't you speak of it like Dad did? I think I finally understood much later—on the day of my own wedding.

There I was, draped in sweltering silk, trying to make sense of all the rituals that assumedly revolved around Vivek and me, and yet needed nothing but a token participation from us. I was surrounded by almost-strangers, who, overnight, would become my family. It was hard not to feel overwhelmed.

My eyes sought you out in the crowd. I don't know if all

mothers have a third eye that keeps a constant watch over their daughters. You definitely did. In the midst of all the ceremonies and their myriad attendant tasks—welcoming guests, exchanging pleasantries, distributing flowers, fetching, instructing, organizing—you turned almost instantaneously to meet my gaze and smile reassuringly.

Newly-wed, the surreal situation of being married, yet not quite able to believe it. I sat in the room that had been Vivek's solitary domain for all these years, wondering how he felt about sharing it. Most of the furniture was new—the double-bed with its side-tables, the dressing table and stool, the tall lamp that stood in a corner. One side of each wardrobe had been emptied to make space for my things. Of Vivek's childhood and young adulthood, only faint traces remained—a couple of framed photographs, the yearly height markings in an unobtrusive corner of the wall, the paint that had come off with a discarded poster. I wished I could see the stuff that had been thrown out, removed, obliterated. That would have probably told me more about my husband than anything in this room.

The change-of-name form lay on the dresser before me, weighed down by a sandalwood jewellery box.

Shweta Kamath.

Four syllables that had been strung together in my mind even before memories were born. The first thing I learned to say to strange, inquisitive adults—'What is your name?', 'Shay-ta Kam-ath.' The name that tested new pens and inaugurated fresh notebooks. The name on eagerly-awaited letters, on un-opened gifts. The name on my certificates, the name below my photograph in the newspaper when I won the inter-school music competition.

The name that was me.

Shweta Nayak. I tried it on for size, rolled it over my tongue, tried to pin it to my reflection in the mirror. It didn't fit.

I've never told you this, but, during those days, I couldn't help but think of Jyoti Didi.

Do you remember when Jyoti Didi moved back into her parents' home after her divorce?

'It ended amicably,' she would say in a well-rehearsed tone.

She was referring, of course, to the practical aspects of the divorce—the division of assets, the settlements. There were things that the lawyers and courts could not divide up equally between them. The hurt, for instance. And the name. Jyothi Amonkar. A well-respected name in Mumbai art circles, it appeared with a trademark flourish at the bottom-right corner of her best paintings. All her life, she would see it everywhere—his name crowding hers, cozying up to hers, jeering at her through the very accomplishments she was most proud of.

No, it wasn't that I was beginning my married life with thoughts of an imminent divorce. Of course not. I was in it for the long haul.

I could adjust to my new family, make compromises, if necessary.

But my name... that was too personal to discard overnight.

When Vivek's mother reacted the way she did, I could have chosen to look around the walls of those spoken words and seen that she, like me, was probably just getting used to my being part of her family.

I never did change my name, and she never could get over it.

That first confrontation has been a tangible presence between us for years now. It has hardened the stands we take on the most trivial of matters.

After my father-in-law's death, Vivek's mother had insisted that she would continue to live in her own home. Staying with us would be inconvenient, she'd said. After all, Annirudh was a teen and wouldn't appreciate having to share his room with his grandmother.

But now that Ani had left for university, we had a room to spare in our two-bedroom apartment.

Even though I had supported the idea of asking her to move in with us, my feelings were mixed. We—Vivek and I—had moved to our own apartment a little before Ani was born. Now, with Ani gone, I was glad for the company, but then, the line between companionship and intrusion was uncomfortably thin. She probably felt pretty much the same.

When we spoke, we took care to keep things at a trivial level. And we always left a back door open—a book, a TV programme, something simmering on the stove—an escape route against the threat of a more intimate conversation.

When Ani went away to college, I knew he was leaving for good. He would visit, of course, but this would never again be his only home. In time, it wouldn't even be 'home', it would be reduced to 'parents' home' or maybe, in a more nostalgic frame of mind, 'childhood home'.

But what I didn't expect was that his absence would hit me with such numbing force. After all, I had always resolved to make time for myself, to do the things I wanted. Learn a new language, perhaps.

Or take up music once again.

A few months back, I came across my old year-book from college.

'Shweta—vivacious, fun-loving, carefree,' read the entry next to my name. 'You could find her engrossed in a crossword puzzle minutes before a gruelling term-end paper. And every Friday night, irrespective of the movie being screened in the Audi, there she would be, exhorting everybody to accompany her. Most of us owe the experience of watching some highly-forgettable movies to her.'

Ma, I don't quite remember the people who wrote this. People who were once my closest friends. But what's worse, I don't remember the person they had written these words about.

I can't recall the last time I saw, or even wanted to see, a complete movie. I have no patience for crosswords. 'Vivacious, fun-loving, carefree'—I doubt that anyone who knows me today would use those adjectives for me.

Ma, you're not alone in losing yourself. Somewhere along the way, we all do.

Dad kept Ma's dementia from me as long as he could, aided to an extent, by the thousand-odd kilometres that separated us. Until it became impossible to hide her deteriorating condition even for the ten-minute duration of our weekly phone calls.

In the evenings, Vivek's mother would sit for hours in the puja-room, deep in prayer, or engrossed in the *Bhagvad Gita*. I envied her the solace she found in religion, something that my atheism kept out of my reach.

Instead, I sat alone at the kitchen table and wrote letters to Ma. I wrote about the ways in which she had let me down and about all the times I had let her down—the former seemed so trivial now; the latter, unforgivable. I wrote about every small incident I could remember, everything I should have shared with Ma while I still could. I wrote, even if it now remained trapped in the mute words of unsent letters.

'You remember those sequined sandals, Shweta?' Dad said on the phone. 'What they meant to me? It's like that. Sometimes her expressions…they tell me… I know… she's in there somewhere…'

Dad and Amit have some sort of a pact to keep the worst from me. That, of course, makes things a hundred times harder. I depend on the inflections in Dad's voice every night to tell me if you have been better or worse that day. I turn to books, projecting your face on the experiences of others. I try to coax out of Google, anything at all that will tell me what you're going through.

Why am I so angry, Ma? At the bottom of everything said and done with a stoic face, there is an undercurrent of resentment at having somehow been betrayed. It is too selfish, too illogical to admit to, but there it is all the same—the face of the petulant child who has been hiding in some corner of me all this while. A child who can never reconcile herself to the reversal of roles…

I can't really tell when my mother-in-law first joined me at the kitchen table, or when our conversations stepped over the invisible boundaries we had drawn and began to make increasingly confident forays into previously untouched territory. Of late, we have stopped tip-toeing around certain topics. Occasionally, the words still run dry. But somehow, even the silence has changed in texture. It no longer stands accusingly in a corner. Instead, it now sits companionably at the table with us.

Sometimes, she reaches over and squeezes my hand. 'Daughter', the gesture seems to say—a word I sorely need to hear. We sit there, saying nothing. Our hands meet at the centre of the table, effortlessly finding the common ground that has long eluded us. We let them do the talking. They chat easily, saying everything that has remained, in all these years, so needlessly unsaid.

••

The House in Ali Bagh

RIKIN KHAMAR

'Thank heavens for the minister-folk of India!' Gungaram muttered as he looked up the half-demolished building.

It had been six months since the government of NCR had declared that all buildings in Delhi that haven't been built with an official permit or have been built over their zoning or height restrictions must be torn down. Of course, the move was denounced by the public as a move to fill the pockets of the developers and the permit officials and was strongly protested, but to no avail. Work had started, and for workers like twenty-seven-year-old Gungaram, who earned less than two thousand rupees a month, this was like being given a job for life as over ninety per cent of the buildings in the capital city of India had sprouted like mushrooms over the last fifty years.

Wiping the thick beads of sweat from his brow, he looked up at the dipping sun. It was nearly time for dinner. Taking a deep breath, he took one last long swing with his pickaxe at the foundation of the building, which crumbled away as if made of sand. Before he could raise his axe once more, he heard the shrill blast of the horn over the loud speaker that signalled to all the day workers to pack up. Instantaneously, dark sweaty men sprung out of the building, like ants pouring out of their hill, each scrambling to flee the broken shell of a building that once used to be a sari shop.

Shaking the loose dirt from his pick, Gungaram walked over to the bundle beneath the lamp-post near the road. Squatting down, he unwound his head-cloth and immediately put a piece of tobacco in his mouth and chewed it angrily. Instead of going straight to his favourite dhaba, where he usually spent the night drinking cheap, locally-brewed liquor out of unwashed bottles and smoked whatever he could; he had to go to the temple today. It was poonam. This of course meant that his wife would go to handover some of his hard-earned money to the only other profession that did less work than the politicians: the priests. He snorted at the thought as he tied the bundle of tools to the end of his pickaxe.

'Gungu!' bellowed a voice behind him. It was Nathu the site supervisor, who always talked to him like he was a worthless insect.

'What?' snapped back Gungaram.

'Tomorrow we start at a new location.'

'Who will finish this place?'

'Bhah! It's so fragile, a fart could topple it. We're getting the bulldozer in tomorrow.'

'Where's the new place?'

'Some house in Ali Bagh. In front of the gate to the abandoned plot in the centre of the street.'

Gungaram knew the place. Without saying he stood up and walked away without a word, as if he were running for the bus or the train. As he turned a corner, he heard the words, 'Don't be late!' echo behind him.

Briskly he made his way along the unpaved side of the road, dodging rocks, sewage and refuse as he made his way towards home—a hut behind a rubbish tip in the old part of the city. All about him irritated horns bleated from every corner as all manners of vehicles, people, and animals, made their way along the metro bypass road. Yet the noise and commotion never bothered him.

It was like the crackling of a broken TV. He did not even see the expensive cars, old taxis, or rickshaws anymore. Not been able to afford one, he had begun to consider them no differently as a villager would consider a cow or an elephant rushing past. Occasionally he would look at the trucks, thinking that if he could save enough money he might be able to get a licence. But he would always dismiss this thought with a shake his head, once he remembered the amount he lost every night in cards and booze.

An unhealthy brown haze developed between the grey purple skies and the glare of the street lights, as the sun finally set. Approaching the flyover, he waited on the side of the road for the lights to turn red, before making a dash across the criss-crossing roads, towards his district. Finally the lights turned green abruptly to red. Gungaram begun to cross, when a fat man on a tiny scooter jumped the lights at the very last minute, and made him bound out of the way. A moment later, the faucet of traffic was again opened by the green light. He scrambled onto an island in the middle of the junction to avoid being mowed down by cars which tore past him.

Gungaram cursed roughly. While he waited for the lights to turn again, it occurred on him that he was no more than a street or so away from the house he was to work on tomorrow. He was suddenly overcome by a queer urge to see what it looked like one last time before it was destroyed; and perhaps imagine what it would look like by the time he and his company was done with it. This thought, along with the thought of his wife and temple, made him turn away from home and walk towards the house in Ali Bagh.

In about fifteen minutes Gungaram stood before the house. Probably a hundred years old, it looked like it had always been empty. Situated right in front of an empty plot that had become wildly overgrown with nettles, the building was like an old unused garbage bin. Little of the original paint was left, and the random blotches of yellow, black, white and brown gave it an infected look, like the skin of a really old man. In the fading light it looked like it would soon crumble away—even without the government's help.

Spitting out whatever tobacco remained in his mouth, Gungaram walked towards the front gate. Strangely, he had the feeling that he had been here before—in that very same spot. It was like an image from a long forgotten dream, or probably somewhere he had stumbled past, while drunk.

Stretching out his hand, he rattled the gate.

The moment he touched the railing, something unexpected happened. A surge of intense euphoria, without boundaries, without understanding, shot through his entire body. It was as if he had ingested a kilo of opium. His eyes were blinded by a white soothing light which seemed to fill him with an energy he had never felt. Crippled by the sensation, he could no longer feel his body. Slowly the light cleared away, and gradually he opened his eyes. Gungaram could hardly believe what he saw. It was a building, whose shape could not be determined, that gave off a radiance that was beyond mere colour—it was pure feeling. It beckoned him to come closer.

Somehow in the next instant he found himself inside. To his astonishment, the walls seemed alive. Images of people, animals, plants, swirled over the walls. It was as if he was looking at the fabric of life. There was no feeling of enclosure—only a sense of space, the kind he had felt whenever he had stepped off the crowded bus to his village, into an empty green field. Total freedom.

He just stood there, for what must have been an eternity, and absorbed as much of this feeling as he could. Gungaram could no longer remember who he was and where he had come from. He only knew for sure that he was here, in this place. A place that connected him to the world unlike any street, telephone or computer would ever do. An understanding seemed to flow into him; filling him with a type of joy, a type of knowledge, he couldn't understand but felt familiar or long forgotten.

The force which impelled him into the house, now called again pulling him in further. Gungaram felt like letting go completely. He slowly released his grip on his body; but something inside him resisted. A small voice or doubt called out to his brain. He began to pull back. He had reached the door, when the scene morphed abruptly. In the next instant, Gungaram found himself outside in the polluted air of Ali Bagh, looking at a decrepit house. As if he had fallen out of the sky, his stomach turned and head spun violently and he dropped to the floor. Eventually, after throwing up violently, he passed out.

It was nearly midnight by the time he awoke. It was cold and with a shiver he picked himself up. Not even daring to look, he stumbled towards the main road. Having reached the main road, the city's natural volume which seemed to have been on mute this entire time, suddenly resumed; and Gungaram put his hands over his ears as he crossed the still busy junction, oblivious to the screeching cars that stopped mere feet away from him, and the angry drivers that swore at him in fury.

Arms wrapped around his chest, Gungaram hypnotically walked on trying to make some sense of what had happened in front of the house. Disorientated, he was unable to articulate by thought or speech what he had experienced, even to himself. He couldn't have been more than a hundred yards from his hut, when a chiming bell stopped him dead in his tracks. Looking up, he saw an old woman hobbling inside a large temple, which looked like every other temple in Delhi, except it was much older and made of carved brown stone, instead of bricks and painted white. A temple from the days without bulldozers or cranes made from the sweat and blood of men. Without thinking he followed her inside.

Ignoring the inhospitable look of the priest, who thought he was a drunk looking for food, Gungaram stared at ceiling and the wide pillars. Covered with gods, demons, dancers, priests, kings, trees and animals, they filled the inside of the temple like vines and flowers do a jungle. Elaborate, intricate, and without purpose, he realised it resembled the inner walls of the house in Ali Bagh, only these were more frozen reproductions of the living, vivid and intense images he had seen.

'Can I help you?' gruffly asked the priest, who was even more concerned as Gungaram had not even had the courtesy to pay his respects to the idol of Lord Shiva which stood at the apex of the temple.

'This temple, how old is it?' asked Gungaram, without taking his eyes off the elaborate carvings.

Stunned by the question, now the priest was sure he was drunk. 'Very old. Now look if you are drunk you might as well go outside. This is a place of enlightenment ... not a dhaba. It was built hundreds of years ago for priests and devotees of the Lord searching for truth and enlightenment—not layabouts looking for free prasad!'

As some attendants bundled him out into the street, the last thing Gungaram remembered was looking at the silhouette of the temple against the backdrop of the ghostly night sky, that for an instant, looked like the shifting outline of the house in Ali Bagh.

The next morning Gungaram awoke with a terrible headache. He looked outside the door of the hut, only a few feet from the mattress on the floor on which he slept. It was the same as always: a thick grey smog lingered in the air as if exhaled by the city smoking invisible cigarettes; while thousands of cars and people flooded past his house as if at twice their usual speed. He could hear his wife cursing loudly and denouncing his presumed all-night drinking on the night of poonam, as she washed their tattered clothes in the disused oil barrel outside. Unable to listen to her tirade anymore Gungaram put on his only other shirt, and left the hut without eating anything or saying a word.

Gungaram had only walked a few minutes when he realized his pickaxe wasn't balanced over his shoulder as usual. It was while trying to recall where it would be, that he suddenly remembered the events of the night before. His mind immediately dismissed last night as the result of too much drinking or not enough sleep over the past few months; but his heart could not do the same. Those piercing sensations he had felt, though diluted by the cold light of day and the putrid smells of the city, could still be felt.

Stopping to avoid hitting a cyclist, Gungaram realised that he stood outside the very same temple from the night before. Recalling the priest's words, a truth dawned on him. He realised that this temple and all the others like it in India, were but mere replicas of that house. Feeble attempts like children to copy a home by making a dollhouse. Efforts by those ancient mystics to feel what he had felt in that house. What he felt, must have been real since others had felt it too, and made these places—places of worship, to inspire, to educate, to connect.

Amidst this revelation, another thought struck Gungaram like a blow to the stomach. The house was to be demolished that very morning.

Like a madman, he began to run as fast as he could towards the house. He must stop them. Ten minutes later he entered Ali

Bagh, bathed in sweat, and hurting all over. Gulping air desperately into his lungs that were punctured with tiredness, Gungaram knew he could not stop, and must keep running. Despite the fog that covered the entire street, including the house, he could see Nathu in the middle of the road shouting at the men to begin their work.

'Stop! Stop!' cried Gungaram almost tripping as he reached the front of the house.

'Gungu you're late! Now get to work!' scolded Nathu.

'We can't! We can't demolish this place.'

Nathu's eyes opened wide. The wildness in Gungaram's voice and appearance, not to mention the nature of his request, made the rest of the men stop and listen.

'Really? May I ask why not? Have you bought it for yourself from lottery winnings?'

'Look Nathu bhai, you have to believe me. There is something about this place! I came here last night and…'

'You came here last night? Listen Gungu, if you have been drinking all night, and think you are going to come here and start babbling instead of working, then you are really in trouble!'

'I'm not drunk!' shouted Gungaram exasperated. 'I really did come here last night and I am telling you this place is different from all the other houses! We can't pull it down.'

'Gungu I am not going to listen to your babble. Get your pickaxe and start working right now!'

Recalling his pickaxe, Gungaram cast a desperate glance to the floor by the gate. It was there. Rushing forward, he picked it up and pushing past the men, stood in front of the gate like an angry guard dog.

'No! I won't let you do it!' he yelled at the top of his voice, lifting his axe threateningly.

'Have you gone mad?' roared Nathu pushing everyone else to

the side. 'If you don't put that down and get out of the way, I am going to have you killed?'

'This is a special place,' cried Gungaram. 'A holy place, a place which is not of this world—and I am not going to let a rat like you take it down!'

'Son of an ass! You insult me? You will never work in Delhi again!' shouted Nathu. 'Look behind you...this pile of bricks is going to fall down anyway; it's not a temple, it's an abandoned house...humph! A holy place indeed!'

Involuntarily, Gungaram looked behind him and was aghast by what he saw. Letting the pickaxe fall from his hands, he slumped to the floor. The fog had thinned somewhat, and having come closer to the house, he saw it was not the same one of the night before. It's colour, shape, structure—everything was different. The house was gone.

•◆

Longing

Women in Love

BISHWANATH GHOSH

P_{rachi}

'Achchha tell me, should I grow my hair?

'Tell na, stop reading that paper! Look at me and tell me. Should I grow my hair?'

'Ufff, I am sick of your answers, "Yes", "Hmmm", "Fine". Do you have an opinion? Now stop reading that paper, will you?'

'Okay, tell me why I should not grow my hair? Give me one good reason. No, no, no, you are not touching me. First answer my question. And by the way, mister, you are not supposed to touch me. That was the deal!'

'And don't you ever cut your nails? Chhee! You don't even trim your moustache. Look in the mirror. You think you look very handsome? You look like Veerappan! There you go again! I told you no touching. Keep your promise like a gentleman.'

'Give me a fag too. You know when I last smoked? That night we went to Ghungroo. Light it for me.... I can never light under a fan.'

'Stupid, I asked you to light my cigarette and not to hold my hand. Besharam! Can't keep your hands off? Ya, ya, don't flatter,

I know my hands are soft and sexy. By the way, I like your hands. Big and manly. Will it hurt if I pull this hair?'

'Ha, ha, ha, ha… That was your punishment for touching Prachi.'

'What kind of a man are you?—screaming just because I pulled a hair! Okay, what do you want for dinner? Kuchh order karen? Or shall I cook? Hey mister, how about you cook for a change?'

'No, no, you are going to cook tonight. Or else you are going back hungry… What? Are you crazy? No way, you are not staying back! No, no, no, you are not staying back.'

'Hey mister, don't mess around with Prachi… Keep your hand away.'

'Nooooo, you are not going there. You are not going anywhere. That tickles, stupid. No, you are not going there… Be a good boy and go to the kitchen. Okay, you read the papers and I will cook. No, no, you are not going there… Okay, okay, put on the FM na, they must be playing Hindi songs now.'

'God, I am listening to this song maybe after ten years! Is that Asha or Lata? Hey mister, now don't take advantage of the song and start doing that. Told you, you are not going anywhere near there… Please na! If you promise to be a good boy I will give you a hug, theek hai? But please keep your hands away. And what about dinner?'

'I am hungry… oh my God, it is 5.45! Will you at least make some breakfast? But there is no bread. Will you get it when the shop opens? No, actually, I will send the watchman. You stay here, with me.'

'What! Are you mad? No, you are not going to office today. Boss? To hell with him. Tell him you are running a fever. Or else I am going to show him these love bites and he will get a fever. What would you prefer, Mr Veerappan?'

Sanjana

'Get me just Sprite. You drink whatever you want to, drunkard that you are.'

'And pick up a packet of chips if you want to. No, not for me. And just before you take the turn you will find a grocery. Will you please pick up some custard powder? Sorry for the trouble.'

'Oh, yes, yes, I know you will take all kinds of trouble today. His Excellency is coming with high hopes. Ha ha ha! Did I tell you that Amit is coming too? He will be here any moment.'

'Hey, hello, don't be an ass. I was kidding. Amit is not in town.'

'Okay, will you just shut up and come?'

'Stop this, will you? I love you, I love you … How many women do you say this to? They might fall for it but I won't, okay?'

'Oh yeah? I am different? And to how many do you say that to?'

'Hey listen, I don't have time for this rubbish. I need to hang up, I can smell the oil burning.'

'Yes, that's my dad. That's my mom and me, and that's my Tippy. She's a pomerian. She's getting blind.'

'No, I will get mine. I hate Gold Flake. Either I smoke Classic, or else I don't smoke. Okay, I'll have a drink with you. A very small one. But please don't drink too much. There's lot of food. The whole morning I have been cooking.'

'Excuse me! I cooked because you have come for the first time not because I love you. Get your head examined, man! And what is this love business? Grow up, man.'

'Yes, I like you. Maybe I also admire you. But what's this love shit? You mad or what? Don't get ideas just because I am nice to you.'

'There, you sulk again. You are impossible, man. Now stop drinking, will you? The alcohol is getting to your head you see. I like R.D. Burman, don't you? I think I have some of his songs, let me check. This is your last drink, by the way. You are not getting anymore. Ha ha ha! What do you mean there is more! I've hidden the bottle. No, no, no, you can't look for it. No, you are not following me. No, you can't search my bedroom. No, please No.'

'These are some R.D. CDs. Back home I have a good collection of his Bengali songs. He would bring out an album every puja. You are not even listening to me. Okay, okay, I will get you your bottle. Drink and die. I will throw away the food.'

'Amit is just a friend, yaar. He is not my boyfriend. Please, for heaven's sake, don't talk about that night. That night there was the whole bunch around. We didn't go to the disco alone. And even if we did, what is your problem? Don't tell me you are jealous. Even if you are, I give a damn.'

'God, one more drink! What meaningful? We can't have a meaningful conversation even while having food. Don't know when you will become a mature adult and stop all this. Don't think I will be after you all your life, telling you not to drink. I really pity your wife, whoever she will be.'

'Oh I love this song. Rekha looks so gorgeous in the movie. Isn't it *Ghar*? And what's his name, yes, Vinod Mehra. How he blows the smoke in her face, and how lovingly she accepts it. Height of romance! Give me a drag, na.'

'No, no, don't shift, just move your legs a bit. I badly need to stretch, been cooking the whole day. And cooking for someone who is not even bothered to eat! Ah, this is another lovely number, my all-time favourite. *Aane wala pal jaane wala hai, ho sake to isme zindagi bita do, pal jo yeh jaane wala hai*—The moment that is arriving is fleeting. So why not live in that moment because tomorrow it will cease. Yes, yes, I know you know the meaning. I was just thinking aloud.'

'Making fun of me? I know very well that this moment I am in the arms of a drunkard. You don't have to remind me of that. Can you re-play the song, please? My hand won't reach there.'

'Who told you I am crying? Sanjana never cries, don't you know that? My eyes are just watery with all the cooking. Hey, I hope the prawn curry does not go bad. It's already, what, eight hours since I made it?'

'Next time remind me to get the CD of *Ghar*. We will watch it together.'

'Give me two minutes, I will just heat up the prawn curry and the daal. No, no, you won't like it cold. Give me just two minutes.'

'Take some more rice, Mr Superman. You've worked really hard. You need the calories. Wait, I'll get the custard. It must be frozen by now. God, it is eleven!'

'Stop it! Let me brush my teeth. God, aren't you tired of me by now?'

'You are like a child when you sleep. You look so cute. Did anyone say that to you before? I kept pushing you off but your hand kept reaching for me. I was up the whole night watching you.'

Amrita

'Why don't you say straightaway I look fat? When did you last see me? Five years? Okay, four. That's a long time. Back then, I was a woman clueless about life. Now I am happily married.'

'Of course you called me fat. What else does pleasantly plump else mean? Anyway, Indian men like plump women only.'

'Plump in the right places? God, have you no shame or what! Talking to me like that? Anyway, let's not discuss me. I am what I am, okay? My husband loves me this way. Any problem?'

'He has gone to Chandigarh for a couple of days. He was on the line before you called. Such a darling he is, calls me every two hours: "Darling, did you have your lunch?" "Darling, are you missing me?" Such a sweetheart!'

'Okay, now you tell me. Why haven't you got married yet? Still chasing women, eh? Do you even remember how many you have slept with?'

'What do you mean by nonsense! The whole world knew what kind of a character you are. Mr Flirt!'

'You never tried it with me? What rubbish! It was I who kept you at an arm's length. If there was one guy who I would not be seen dead with it was you! Such a rogue!'

'Okay, okay, fine. Won't talk about all that. So tell me, why no marriage yet? You could have easily found one from your harem. Ha! Ha! Ha! Anyway, good to hear from you. But listen, find someone soon. It is nice to be married.'

'Of course I'm happy. He is a sweet guy, yaar. Very sweet. First, in the morning he makes tea for me, can you imagine that? He clears the dishes, pays the bills, everything! Miss him so much, poor guy.'

'You got to go? Okay, will catch up sometime soon. And hey, thanks for calling. Yeah, take care, bye!'

'Yeah, he came back two days ago. Yes, from Chandigarh. Do you ever pay attention when I talk? Achchha listen, am I disturbing you? Please let me know whenever you think is not the right time to talk. You are the busy man.'

'Never too busy for me? Nice to hear that, Mr Flirt. But it is not going to work with me, okay? And don't forget, I am now a happily-married woman. Achha, I am still curious to know why haven't you got married yet.'

'Find a girl for you? Why should I do that? What happened to your harem? They all ditched you or what?'

'Who will marry you, yaar? And you want me to find a girl for you! Have I gone mad or what? That poor girl—she will come after me with a knife. But let's hear what kind of a girl you want.'

'Okay…okay…go on, go on… Ah, smart, intelligent, well-read,

sense of humour, same wavelength as you, and what else Mr Flirt?'

'And good at sex? Ha! Ha! Ha! You can't think of anything beyond that, can you? Let me tell you, marriage is not all about sex. It is a lot more. I don't know if you will understand.'

'Achha listen, why I called was... I wanted to tell you not to call me after six.'

'I know, I know you don't keep calling. I am just telling you. After six he is back home. Feels a bit awkward.'

'Yeah, he knows we talk once in a while. I tell him everything.'

'I had thought I would never call you again. Never, never again. But stupid me.'

'What do you mean by what happened? You should know what happened?'

'Do you expect me to tell you everything? Do you want me to say, "Hey, it is my birthday, please wish me?" I thought you would call.'

'See, I told you, you never pay attention to what I say.'

'What sorry? Fuck your sorry. No, no, no, this is unpardonable.'

'No, no, no, don't darling me now. I am very pissed. You and your bloody work! I hate you!'

'No, yaar, what does it take to make one call? You know he is not home at that time. Anyway, now I know you don't care.'

'No, no, no, it's okay. Leave it. No, leave it.'

'Now why do you want to know that? I am not telling you.'

'No, why do you want to know what I did when you didn't even remember to call me?'

'No, nothing much. We went out for dinner. He had already ordered a birthday cake. And guess what, he gave me diamond earrings. Can you believe that? Such a sweetheart he is. Anyway, it was your call I was waiting for.'

'No, don't darling me now. I am very pissed.'

Effacing Memories

PARITOSH UTTAM

From the recesses of the mahogany cabinet out flew Lucy's memories: cards with time-blunted edges, letters as yellow as decayed teeth, photographs whose colours were mere ghosts of the originals...but not the photograph she wanted. She searched frantically, as if another moment's delay could not be borne; as if one minute more over the forty years since she had seen him last, or over the one month since his death, would be a minute too many.

She had no way to determine the precise instance in those forty years in which his face escaped her memory. Perhaps, it hadn't vanished with one brutal wrench, but rather faded away like the colours on those photographs, or disappeared piecemeal, like the eclipse of the sun: first the hair, then the eyes, the nose, the mouth. Now she recalled nothing.

The realization of her faulty memory had come suddenly, when Sophie gave her the news. They were sitting in the evening, as was their daily custom, in the strange, solitary seats that dotted Joggers' Park, watching their respective grandchildren playing and running. Lucy could make out the accusatory tone in Sophie's voice, coming from a few feet away. Antony had died a month ago, of cancer, alone in his reclusive bungalow in Mussoorie, noticed only by the milkman two days later, and mourned by none. He had died with Lucy's name on his lips.

Lucy recognized the last bit immediately as Sophie's contribution, for if he died alone, who could know his last words?

But she did not contradict Sophie, because his death was a fact she could not deny. The guilt that she had managed to evade for so long, despite Sophie's muted censure, finally clung to her. And now her memory obstructed her in expiating that guilt.

When she returned home from the park, barely a ten-minute walk away, even at their doddering pace, she left her granddaughter watch cartoon network and set about searching for his photograph. An uproar of howls and shrieks interspersed with the tinkling laughter of her granddaughter came from the living room.

How blissful it was, Lucy imagined, to be able to believe in those cartoons in which bombs exploded and people fell from skyscrapers but no one ever died, and nobody's face was ever obliterated. Where was the photograph, now? It had to be in one of the secret drawers of the cabinet because she remembered caching it there but not taking it out.

She remembered other things. He had kind eyes, but that she remembered only as a fact she told him once, and not how his eyes actually were. They were brown and kind, black and kind, or even green—she could believe anything now.

Of their photograph she could recall every single detail, from his neck downwards. He had worn a light shirt, with narrow dark stripes; sleeves rolled to just above the elbows, giving him a debonair air, and dark trousers. His left arm wrapped her shoulder in his embrace. They had gone all the way to a photo studio in Colaba and posed with the prop of a red Chevrolet in the backdrop.

The photographer recognized their shy affection for each other and wished them luck. How could she remember all these details, and yet forget his face?

The photograph had to be in the cabinet because it was the only one she couldn't bring herself to burn. When she knew she couldn't marry him, she had destroyed all their letters and photographs save that one, hoping that the removal of all those sweet souvenirs would, with time, pave the way for those which lingered in her mind.

There were reasons, important then, but which the passage of time had made trivial, and certainly not as insurmountable as she had thought at first, though by the time she realized that, it was too late. Parental approval was paramount, at least to her. On the face of it, her father did not have any reason to object to Antony, for he was a Goan Catholic like them. But apparently, his family was not as respected as theirs was, back in Goa. Later, Lucy understood that it was only her father's ego that prevented him from accepting her choice: how could his daughter choose someone without his knowledge and permission?

Antony and Sophie, her staunch friend even forty years back, failed to convince her that all she needed was a little pluck to face her father, but she was too timid. Instead, she married the man her father picked. To be fair to her father and her husband, it was not a bad match: she had been happy, or at least she had no reason to be unhappy with her marriage that lasted for thirty-five years until her husband's death five years ago. They had their own house, children and grandchildren. What more could she expect?

So you move on, Lucy cried, flailing her arms at Sophie to counter her incriminating glances, you move on as life does. You don't get stuck in a time warp. You don't take a vow you will not marry anybody else. And you certainly don't keep that vow until you die.

It was his tribute to his love for you. He didn't ask you for anything in return. He just didn't want to debase his love by sharing it with someone else, Sophie told her, letting her expression imply whatever she had left unsaid. The least he deserves are your tears.

Another round of explosions and laughter from the living room brought her mind back to the cabinet. Lucy remembered, all at once, an innermost chamber, a recess within a recess. The photograph was there. She drew it out and gasped in horror.

Her picture was intact, and so was his arm around her, but not his face. That side of it was nibbled away by termites or silverfish, in a grotesque parody of her memory, as if time and nature both had conspired in forcing her to pay homage to a man who would remain faceless forever.

•◆

Trial and Error

NAMAN SARAIYA

I woke up to the sound of a whirling, creaking fan against the usual sounds that morning. It was a strange feeling, considering that my memory had been failing me, minute by minute, since the time I had opened my eyes to the dim, sunlit room. After a few seconds of looking around, I realized a cheap, thin blanket was covering my naked, cold self. My vision, devoid of glasses, spotted a bottle of what looked like alcohol, on the table placed at the foot of the bed. The scene, from the night before, was falling in place, like the pieces of a jigsaw. As I lay down again, looking to my right, she turned around which explained the shifty nature of the bed.

And then, her hair fell back…

I was thirteen, when enlightenment of a different kind dawned on me, courtesy a senior at school. This, I later believed, was the very blessing of being at a boarding school—sex education and a sound knowledge of abusive language came free of cost, since everyone's guess was as good as yours. Maybe this was what all-round education was all about. Having begun my second year at a residential school, tucked away in some corner of Nainital, I missed her more than home. Strange as it was—what could two eleven-year-olds have possibly shared, to have me thinking about it, two years on, that it still played in my head. But, that was the truth—a glaring truth that haunted me through my teenage years and does so, even now—in my adulthood. As it happened, that afternoon was the last I saw of her for a long, long time to come.

It was just one of those days during my final year of college at Pune, when Facebook was quite the rage. We all kept logging in and out every fifteen minutes to check notifications—which also doubled up as fodder for conversations and gossip—since we all 'were so bored in life.' Ah, 'bored in life'—how grammatically incorrect that was, my remedial grammar faculty had once professed! This time I logged in after just two minutes and there was 'one new notification.' Facebook had begun confusing me, despite the time I spent on it, owing to its continual change and experimentation with the user interface. That one new notification was a friend request, which had just come in from Zoya Contractor. Ah! There she was, I thought to myself. The joys of social media—God bless these blokes!

Zoya Contractor, the girl who had caught my attention for years together, had now found me on Facebook of all places! A childhood sweetheart, the daughter of my mother's friend and my first contact with womankind—all packaged into this one being, so perfect and beautiful, was now, finally, in touch with me! That one meeting, on a sunny May afternoon, so clearly etched in my mind, remained a vivid memory for years to come and was also the starting point of our conversations for months after we got in touch that day. The terrace swing, the animated movie on the computer, some homemade popcorn, shy and controlled laughter, lack of eye contact, holding hands and a lot of nervousness. It was this, which kept playing in my head, like a scene from a movie.

Over and over again…

Things began to pick up pace over the next few months. The women in my life came and went, like local trains at Churchgate in Mumbai, but she didn't budge. My childhood love, if I could take the liberty of calling her that, was back and how. But no, it wasn't love this time. We had moved on to become absolutely different people who still understood each other (or liked to believe so). Over STD calls—which burnt holes in our pockets—we learnt of our differences and similarities but retained our bond. The long-lost friendship, relationship was blossoming (again?) and I made a million plans to visit her in Hyderabad. Why did her parents have to shift? Had they stayed back, in Calcutta, life would have been simpler, but not the same I guess.

So, with great difficulties and one break-up with the hottest girl in college, my regained and resurfaced bond with Zoya blossomed fully. And to think it was ten years since I had last seen her was more dramatic than depressing. Several plans to pay each other a visit and so on and so forth kept doing the rounds, but nothing of the sort happened. College attendance was always an issue for me. Despite our parents' awareness—something essential in our society—nothing worked out. And this was when problems started between us. And after that, one baseless argument which evolved into a spat, it was all over (or so I thought). Zero contact. Maybe a one-off text message every few months, and that was it.

Three years had passed since that fight with Zoya. After graduating from college, I decided not to go back to Calcutta and stayed on in Pune, finding shelter in lame excuses such as adjustment issues back home and how the city had no scope for progress career-wise. I was now working with a daily newspaper as a freelance features writer and photographer. Since my freelance assignments playing in my head, alone did not fulfil my monetary and lifestyle needs, I also directed theatrical productions on and off and conducted workshops in colleges. Keeping myself busy had made life easier and not having committed to a single woman in the last two years had made life even easier. That was when I took a week off from work to visit Nainital—to please my camera's lens, visit school and give another shot at my incomplete novel.

When I reached this town, which we, at school, often referred to as home or even heaven on earth, a heady feeling began coursing through my body. I was glad that it did. The first thing I generally did, after dumping my bags in the hotel room, was take a walk down Bhutia Market, Flats and then Mall Road before settling down for lunch at one of the many restaurants that featured on my 'favourites' list. And the lunch, more often than not, comprised a thirteen-year-olds' favourites—spring rolls or momos, half a tandoori chicken and cold coffee followed by gulab jamun. And that's exactly what I did that day. However, this time I had company—my trusted Nikon D5000. All of a sudden, I wanted to capture every single thing I had seen over the years.

Once again I said to myself, 'Ah! God bless technology!'

On my third or fourth night at Nainital, I was walking down the extreme end of Mall Road, with one hand dug deep into my pocket. Since I felt cold at any given point of the year, I lit a cigarette as an excuse to keep myself warm. After crossing most of the familiar locations and observing some changes, I realized I had been smiling all along. A smile I had not smiled in the longest time, not since I had met Zoya and shared a cup of coffee over Skype. But that virtual meeting had taken place a few years ago and, I hadn't spoken to her since then. And there, thoughts of her struck me again, almost a year after I had last thought of her.

Oh, nostalgia. And, how it was such a bitch.

I walked on with thoughts of Zoya, which in my opinion wasn't playing in my head, like the best thing but it did bring a smile to my face. I gave up the playing in my head, like mental struggle, trying to stub out thoughts of Zoya with what I realized was my third cigarette. I stopped at one of the benches on Mall Road, one with a streetlight, and sat down after assuring myself that there weren't too many people around. All of a sudden I got up and walked to a street cart selling ice cream to get one for myself. I didn't stop to consider how ironic that was, considering I had just smoked three cigarettes to keep myself warm. As I paid the vendor and turned around, I bumped into someone. As filmy as the scene was, I didn't see the face and bent down to help pick up the contents of the fallen bag.

Why? Why? I don't understand. Karma, it is. Zoya Contractor, it is.

What happened next was quite the expected—shock, surprise and a loss of words. And then over the next couple of minutes, various attempts at conversation were made. I alternated between cursing and thanking my stars. But this was it. I was faced with reality at an unexpected time and an unexpected town I was then reminded of a cheesy line from a Shahrukh Khan movie about how the universe conspires to help you get what you want if you truly wish for it. But, what if you haven't wished for it? What then? Did anyone have an answer for that? I'm guessing no. Then, you just call it plain bad luck. Or perfect timing. Oh, I needed to get a hold of my life. Life? No. That was pretty much sorted. It were my thoughts which needed control at that moment.

And, then it was time for dinner. With her.

Fast as this was moving, we decided to take dinner to her hotel room. On the way, I learnt she was in Nainital for some environmental research and that her work was to begin in a couple of days. She confessed that the town reminded her of me, considering I went on and on about it but also agreed with most things I had to say. Plentiful revelations and confessions later, (or was it before?) a bottle of inexpensive wine joined us and in my head, I knew this was not a good thing. But then again, men are from Mars—if you know what I mean. A meeting after more than a decade, a makeshift dinner in a shoddy hotel room with a creaking fan, tables arranged randomly and two people resurfacing a long-lost relationship—this had turned out to be a story worth telling.

Soon enough, we were cleaning up, which was more like brushing everything aside, in between intimate moments. But, it wasn't right by my plan of action. 'Don't commit', I kept saying in my head, but the heart overruled every single time. Swigs of cheap wine straight from the bottle, patterns of smoke and the taste of tobacco, undressing and the smell of her earthy skin, passion and the heat overriding the weather outside—it summarized that night or the bits of it that I could recall. Love cannot save you from your own fate I had once heard someone say. Well, if this was my fate, I'd like to have lived that moment of fate, a thousand times over. Zoya Contractor and I, meant to be or not, I could not tell. But, in the same room, I did not want to say.

And that was that, but this was not it.

'Love and sex are two things that really hang people up.'

Cate Blanchett as Bob Dylan—from the motion picture I'm Not There, 2007

•◆

Driving Down the Memory Lane

KUNAL DHABALIA

I glanced left and saw my wife dozing off as I drove across the rural landscape rendered hauntingly beautiful by the moonlight. It had taken many fights over the last few days and a trade-off on my side to take the car instead of the bike, but eventually I was able to convince her to drive the 200 odd kilometres to attend a family function. She had carried the sombre mood with her into the car as well, with neither of us able or willing to lighten the atmosphere. The drive continued to be tense until she finally fell asleep.

As the car sped along, the landscape turned monochrome and I began to reminisce about the times when the drives used to be enjoyable, when at every opportunity I would kick-start another night long expedition. One particular memory came flooding back.

Working long hours at office was not my strength, and so normally I would be out the door by 6.00 to 7.00 p.m. This time, however, an impending release had compelled me to stay back till 11.00 p.m.

Just as I was leaving, I saw her—standing outside the exit gate, waiting for an auto. I knew that she worked on the same floor as mine, and that her desk was two cubicles away from mine, but apart from that I did not even know her name. On seeing her, the romantic in me wanted to stop immediately and offer her a lift, but then the geek in me kicked in and I felt 'odd' about offering a lift to a girl I did not even know and I drove past. About hundred meters later, my conscience pricked me about leaving a colleague alone on the side of the road late at night. As if it had a mind of its own, my bike completed a U-turn, and I was back at the exit gate.

'Can I drop you somewhere?' I asked and hoped she recognized me.

'That would be really helpful, but I'd hate to bother you,' she replied, confirming that she had indeed recognized me.

'I don't mind at all, and anyway at this time with almost zero traffic on the roads, the drive would be refreshing rather than a nuisance,' I said.

She was hesitant, and looked around. 'I'll get an auto.'

'I doubt you would find an auto that easily at this time, and even if you find one you'd be charged exorbitant rates. If I leave you here Aman would never let me live it down.'

'Aman? Who is that?' she asked.

I smiled. 'That would be me.'

'That was a pathetic way of introducing yourself.' She was smiling as she hopped onto the bike and said, 'I am Shikha.'

'Nice to meet you. By the way where should I drop you?' I started the bike.

'I live in Banjara Hills,' she replied. 'And where do you stay?'

'I stay in Hi-Tech City, a kilometre away.'

'Now you are making me feel guilty again, because of me you are going so much out of your way.' She sounded a bit blue.

'Hey don't worry about it at all, driving at night is my mantra for relaxation,' I said.

'Ohh, that is interesting! Aren't you afraid?' She seemed genuinely interested.

'Afraid of what? The empty roads? And for the record till date I've not encountered a single ghost asking for lift on the road,' I said smiling at the image.

I felt there were more questions coming forth and I was proved right. 'Don't you get in trouble anytime with the cops?' she asked.

'Actually every time I am flagged down we end up having a nice chat since I've all the documents, and am never drunk while driving. Usually the cops are also bored at night and are always up for a bit of chit-chat,' I told her.

'But…' she still seemed to have doubts about the safety of night-time driving.

'The biggest problem I've faced till now is a flat-tire. I had to leave my bike on the road-side for the whole night, while I caught a call centre cab to my home. That was a bad night. I was dead worried about my bike being stolen.' I shuddered remembering that night.

'You seem so attached to your bike, the way you talk about your bike it almost seems you treat it as a human being.' I could almost hear the smile in her voice.

'For me this bike is my most prized possession. And after all it is only the bike that provides me company on all my drives,' I explained.

'Oh, so you drive alone.' It was more of a statement rather than a question.

'Yep, I drive with only my bike for company. All my friends are sane enough not to sacrifice their sleep for a drive around in the night,' I said.

'So the solitude is forced, not desired.'

I shrugged. 'Everything depends on the company. I love driving alone, and I love driving while talking to someone, and actually, I am really enjoying this drive with you.'

'Good to hear that, even I am enjoying this late night drive. I could easily make a habit out of it.' Again, I could imagine smiling as she said that.

'Great!' was all I could manage when the perfect thing to say at that time would have been, 'I could help you. Give me your number. I'll call you whenever I am going for a drive. Then let's see if you have an appetite for losing sleep whilst roaming around the near empty streets of Hyderabad.' This thought bubble hovered over my head for a while and as I was scrounging for any remnants of courage left to say that, the geek in me whipped a pin out and pricked the thought bubble. Any subsequent thoughts on these lines were quashed by the aforementioned socially awkward introverted geek.

A few minutes of uncomfortable silence—at least for me—like followed.

'You can stop here. I live in the white building near the ice cream shop,' she directed.

I stopped the bike and bid her adieu. I think she knew what I wanted to say, and waited an extra moment on the stairs giving me another chance. She soon realized I was too afraid to say a thing and went in.

As I came back to the present, I looked over to the warring, but sleeping wife and wondered—what would have happened had I gathered the courage to say those words? Had I asked her out? Would my life have been different then, would this drive have been more enjoyable?

I guess I'll never know.

•◆

A Mood for Love

PARITOSH UTTAM

Ruchi came out of the bath, refreshed. A white turkey towel coiled around her head turban-fashion. A bigger bath towel hugged her tightly below the armpits. She went across the room to shut the window, leaving behind progressively fainter watery patterns of arched feet. Almost at once, she was aware of the tang in the air.

She leant over the breast-high windowsill, peering upward beyond the awning. A few straggling clouds floated in the distance, as if uncertain whether to approach or disperse. Their ambiguous nature was reflected in their colour too—neither a benign white nor an ominous black—but a sober, sombre grey. But the clouds didn't really matter, for she could sense the as-yet-unfallen rain.

She saw it in the bougainvillea leaves quivering in anticipation of the raindrops that would rock them with their weight. She felt it in the cool breath that caressed her bare shoulders, and smelt it in the mixture of dampness and freshness the wind bore. The panic of eternal longing wrenched her heart so tightly that she had to shut her eyes. Wouldn't she like something more tangible than the wind on her shoulders? A pair of brown, unseen hands perhaps, the fingers traversing her tingling skin from shoulder-tip to nape to shoulder-tip? And then the warm hands would grip her shoulders from behind in a gentle crush, drawing her back so that she had no option but to rest her head against his chest and she would look up and see... what?

He had a thousand faces and he had no face. He had curly, short, wavy, straight long hair; he had coal black, fiery, kind dark brown, or even timid blue eyes; he had clean-shaven granite cheekbones; his stubble covered his tapering chin.

Ruchi heaved a sigh that was much, much older than her eighteen years, a sigh carrying the burden of generations of insuperable human loneliness. It scared her, and she quickly shut the window and pulled her chemise down over her towel-turbaned head after a brief struggle. She heard the TV on in the sitting room.

'What are you watching, Prachi?' Ruchi asked. Her sister looked comfortably settled slumped low in the bean bag, her feet resting on the coffee table. The hemline of her maxi brushed the floor.

'*Qayamat Se Qayamat Tak*,' she answered, without moving her eyes off the TV screen. 'Rahul called,' she added a minute later. 'Twice. I said you were in the bath. He will call again.'

Ruchi grunted an acknowledgement, staring at the screen herself. How young Aamir looked then! She dragged a chair to the coffee table and settled down, Prachi-like, though she was sure she was not as comfortable as Prachi was.

'Haven't seen it for a long time,' Ruchi said, in justification.

In return, Prachi gave her a short, puzzled look and turned away.

She knows I'm feeling strange, Ruchi thought. She felt a sudden skittish urge to play hopscotch. The ache inside her persisted.

'They make a nice pair, don't they? Aamir and Juhi, how young and innocent they both look,' Prachi said, while Ruchi was trying to arrange her chemise that had ridden up her thighs. It was such a bother trying to sit ladylike, she thought, and then gave up the attempt realising there was only Prachi in the room.

The shriek of the cordless phone startled her. Prachi took it up and said, 'For you.' Ruchi started again. Damn it. Why was she feeling so jumpy? She noticed a bemused twist on Prachi's face. Now Prachi would think she was getting high-strung about Rahul.

Could he be…? Were those his fingers that played on her shoulders?

'Hello, Rahul?'

'Sure it's me. So how are you? I have been trying to reach you for hours. When did…?'

Prachi was waving her arms at her frantically motioning her away towards the door.

'I can't hear the TV,' she said.

Ruchi opened the door that looked out onto the garden and sat on the doorstep, glad that the hedge along the boundary that separated their house from the neighbour's was tall enough to hide her from view. She was also glad that her parents had heeded her suggestion and let Prachi and her choose an independent house to live-in, instead of the tiny apartment students usually stayed in.

Serving in the Indian Foreign Service, her father rarely spent more than a couple of weeks in India. He had to move countries and even continents every two to three years. This, her parents decided, was playing havoc with their children's education, and so it was in their best interest if they stayed put in India to pursue their studies, in their hometown Hyderabad. Of course, to assuage their recurring guilt of staying away from their children, they seldom refused anything Ruchi or Prachi wished, and Ruchi had learnt to exploit that weakness years ago.

The wind had become stronger. It perforated the sheer fabric of her chemise, ran through her body and whipped up the turbulence in her heart. She felt a centripetal force on her chest, imagining it would cave in under the pressure any moment. It hurt, by God, it hurt.

C'mon Rahul, be nice, say something nice. I could love you. I could love anybody now. What was he saying?

'… you tell me you would return from Delhi today. But you were here three days back. Ashish told me he saw you at the Minerva Coffee House. Why didn't you tell me? Why did you lie?'

Oh Rahul, Rahul. Ruchi looked sadly at the mouthpiece. How does it matter now? It was so long ago, one week back. How do I remember what I said, or why I said it? God knows what mood I was in. Or maybe I can remember if I try. But not now, not now. Not when I'm in this mood of longing, of love.

'I'm sorry Rahul, I don't remember.'

'Don't remember! I remember. It was that evening we had a meal at KFC and then we watched *Avatar* at Prasad IMAX, when I asked… but… you said that…'

Please Rahul, please. Don't quibble. Not now. Can't you see the fallen white and pink bougainvillaea flowers fluttering round and round on the ground, in this heady wind? Can't you feel it? This is the only time it actually feels romantic in Hyderabad, after all these months of heat and dust and dryness. Can't you smell that it is going to rain?

'It doesn't matter now, Rahul.'

'It does matter. It hurts me. I don't know why you treat me so. You know how I feel about you. How much I love you…'

That's better. But not in that whining voice. Why do you need so many words? Just look up and see the darkening pregnant rainclouds. There! A drop fell on my foot just now. In a little while, you can smell the fresh upturned muddy earth. You don't have to talk. If you love me, you will come here to me.

'…I live and die for you, Ruchi. You are the only person I love. I'll do anything for you. I'm crazy about you. Why don't you love me? Please Ruchi, say you love me…'

How banal can you get! Don't whine, don't plead, don't beg, and don't talk. Come. I want to feel your breath on my cheeks, on my nape, not your panting over a telephone line. I cannot transmit my love through a bunch of electromagnetic waves or a strand of copper wires.

'Say something, Ruchi. I want to talk to you. Can I come over and see you?'

Finally. She leant her head against the doorjamb looking with contentment at the patch of ground at her feet that began to darken rapidly as bigger, fatter drops smacked the earth with a mini explosion. How long would he take to come here? Fifteen minutes? Twenty?

'Oh, no. It's raining. Of all the… I hope it stops soon. I'll come over as soon as it stops.'

Ruchi looked at the phone with disbelief, as though she was holding something disgusting. As soon as it stops? For God's sake, why does he want the rain to stop? It has just started.

'…never know when these rains end, once they start. If it takes long, I'll come later in the evening or tomorrow…'

Later? Tomorrow? When was tomorrow? Tomorrow she wouldn't feel this way. Now! She felt the wetness on her cheeks and she knew it wasn't because of the rain. She was faintly aware of a squeaking in her ears, Rahul's voice from somewhere far, far away. He was still talking. Hadn't he finished yet?

'…tomorrow… meet tomorrow…'

Ruchi looked back at the TV. Prachi was in exactly the same posture as before, her eyes glued to the screen.

'No, not tomorrow,' Ruchi said. What did Prachi find so interesting there? Aamir was chasing Juhi among eucalyptus trees or was it Juhi chasing Aamir... hard to say. Did Prachi find love on the TV screen as enchanting as the love she herself yearned for?

'Why not tomorrow?'

She thought hard of something to shut him up.

'I'm not well. I've some problems.'

'What problems?'

'Oh, I can't tell you. Why don't you understand? Some problems playing in my head, like girls have.'

'Oh.'

Ruchi smiled sadly. It always worked. Now he would act the chivalrous gentleman.

'Yes, I understand. I'm sorry. I'll meet you later, when you are... are okay. Take care. Bye. Love you.'

'Bye.'

Yes, perhaps love in two dimensions was better than in three, provided the missing dimension was reality. Ruchi looked out again.

It had begun to rain steadily.

'Hey Ruchi,' Prachi yelled from inside. 'Come here fast. You are missing the best scene in the movie.'

•◆

Contributors

VRINDA BALIGA

Vrinda lives in Hyderabad. Her short stories have appeared in various literary journals and magazines like *Temenos, flashquake, The Shine Journal, Long Story Short, Rose & Thorn* and *Cezanne's Carrot.* She is a prize winner in the Katha Fiction Contest 2010 organized by India Currents.

More at www.facebook.com/vrinda.baliga

HASMITA CHANDER

Hasmita sometimes wishes she could live in a fictional world and she does, through the stories she reads and writes. She inhabits the real world in Mumbai, where she writes, edits and conducts creative writing workshops. Her writing has travelled wider than she has, published in seven countries and online, over the last decade.

More at http://www.hasmitachander.com

KUNAL DHABALIA

Kunal grew up in Raipur, resides in Hyderabad and has been blogging for over six years. He loves getting lost in a sea of words, be it writing or reading. He observes the people around him and weaves stories about their lives. A software professional, he enjoys travelling and photography, but believes his true calling lies in writing.

More at http://kunal.wordpress.com; www.facebook.com/kunal.dhabalia

AHMED FAIYAZ

Ahmed Faiyaz grew up in Bangalore and now lives in Dubai. He is a strategist by profession, with a number of years in Management Consulting behind him. He's a book and film addict, and apart from reading books and watching cinema of all genres, he is a passionate writer. His first book, *Love, Life And All That Jazz*, published in April 2010 is a popular bestseller across major cities. Grey Oak also released, *Another Chance*, his second full-length novel, and *Strangers*, his anthology of twenty-one short stories in February 2011. He enjoys long getaways in the mountains or to secluded beaches, where he reads a book a day. He is also one of the founding members of Grey Oak Publishers and Grey Oak Foundation.

More at www.ahmedfaiyaz.in and www.twitter.com/ahmedfaiyaz

ABHA IYENGAR

Abha is a poet and writer. Her work has appeared in *Mannequin Envy, Muse India, Bewildering Stories, Up The Staircase, Danse Macabre, The Fabulist* and many others. Her story, 'The High Stool', was nominated for the Story South Million Writers Award. Her poem-film, 'Parwaaz', has won a Special Jury prize in Patras, Greece. She has a published poetry collection titled, *Yearnings*.

Her stories have most recently been selected for *A Rainbow Feast: New Asian Short Stories, The Asian Writer, Vaani* and *The*

Unisun: Reliance Time Out anthologies. She has received the Lavanya Sankaran Writing Fellowship for 2009-2010.

More at www.abhaiyengar.com, www.abhaencounter.blogspot. com, www.facebook.com/abha.iyengar and twitter.com/abhaiyengar

MALATHI JAIKUMAR

Malathi Jaikumar, a Chennai-based freelance writer, was earlier a senior sub-editor with *Indian Express*, Delhi; Deputy Head Press and Public Affairs, British High Commission, New Delhi. She was awarded the MBE. After retirement, she worked briefly as a Communications Consultant for UNDP, doing post-Tsunami advocacy work. She was awarded the first prize in the Femina All India Short Story Competition and in Drafting Competition for Locally Engaged Staff in British Missions worldwide.

RIKIN KHAMAR

Rikin Khamar is a London-born author, whose first book *The Lotus Queen* was released in December 2010. He also writes poetry and indulges in photography and painting. Rikin currently lives with his family in Dubai.

More at www.rikinkhamar.com

SAHIL KHAN

Sahil is a lifestyle activist, foodie, music lover and designer. Though agnostic, he likes to believe that he is an experiment of God. He runs an online magazine, *TheTossedSalad.com*, and an egg specialty restaurant in Yolkshire. He is also a food columnist for *Mid-Day*.

More at http://facebook.com/sahilk, http://sahilk.tumblr. com, http://twitter.com/sahilk

KAINAZ MOTIVALA

Kainaz Motivala is an upcoming Indian film actress and model who acted in *Wake Up Sid* and *Paathshaala* where her performance was well-received. She has also appeared in a number of commercials for Mc Donalds, Uninor, Sony Pix and Videocon, among others. Kainaz is passionate about writing, and is a former journalist. She has had stints with The Express Group and The Times Group and was a features writer with *Hair Magazine* before her foray into films as an actor.

She always had a liking for the performing arts, having trained under Shiamak Davar for six years. While in Jai Hind College, Kainaz participated in a number of cultural events and won a couple of dance competitions at the inter-collegiate level. Apart from acting and dancing, Kainaz enjoys reading and spending time with her canine friends. In her spare time, she volunteers at the Welfare of Stray Dogs. Kainaz is a globetrotter and loves to travel and experience new cultures. She speaks English, Hindi, German, Gujarati, French and Marathi.

More at www.twitter.com/kainazm and www.greyoak.in/urbanshots

BISHWANATH GHOSH

Bishwanath Ghosh grew up in Kanpur and now lives in Chennai. He is an accomplished travel writer and an Associate Editor with *Times of India*, Chennai. Bishwanath's first travelogue, *Chai Chai*, was published in 2009. It was a bestseller in many centres and garnered good reviews. His second novel *Tamarind City: Where Modern India Began* was published in 2012. He is passionate about writing and is an avid reader.

More at http://bytheganges.blogspot.com

PRATEEK GUPTA

Prateek doles out advice to multinational corporations as a profession and generally expects to be paid for it. Apart from his full-time job in the consulting industry, he dabbles in writing fiction and non-fiction for newspapers, magazines and his blog. An avid reader and writer by passion, a social media junkie, and a technology enthusiast, he has lived almost all over India during his constant stint and is now based out of Bangalore.

More at http://prats.co.in

PARITOSH UTTAM

Paritosh Uttam is a Pune-based software engineer. He holds a Bachelor's degree from IIT Madras and a Master's from IISc Bangalore. Apart from writing and reading modern literary fiction, he is enthused by internet routing protocols, web search-engine optimization techniques, Nifty and mutual funds, crosswords and anagrams, cricket and table tennis. Several of his short stories have been published in various magazines, newspapers and e-zines.

More at www.paritoshuttam.com

NAMAN SARAIYA

Naman is a novelist, experimental photographer and the Editor of *TheTossedSalad.com*.

More at http://twitter.com/namansaraiya and http://namansa-rikasaraiya.wordpress.com

•◆